CASTLE
TOURMANDYNE

Also by Monica Hughes

CASTLE TOURMANDYNE

Monica Hughes

HarperCollins*Publishers*Ltd

First published in hardcover by HarperCollins Publishers Ltd: 1995
First paperback edition: 1996

Canadian Cataloguing in Publication Data

Hughes, Monica, 1925-
  Castle Tourmandyne

ISBN 0-00-648083-7

I. Title.

PS8565.U34C3 1995   jC813'.54   C95-930447-9
PZ7.H84Ca 1995

---

96 97 98 99 ❖ OPM 10 9 8 7 6 5 4 3 2

Printed and bound in the United States

*For Bob and Gerry Bell,
of the Strathacona Model and Toy Museum,
who make magic with paper*

CASTLE
TOURMANDYNE

ONE

Marg woke up with the sun shining in her eyes and remembered that it was her birthday. Twelve years old at last. Only one year away from being in her teens. She bounced up in bed, saw the mound in the other bed and her happy mood vanished, as if a cloud had slid across the sun. Cousin Peggy!

The depressing thing was that she'd really been looking forward to Peggy's visit. Aunt Christine and Uncle Terry, who owned a swanky antique store in Toronto, had to go on a buying trip to Thailand and couldn't take their daughter with them.

"Poor Peg," Marg had sympathised. "How rotten for you."

"I don't care one bit. Travel's boring anyway," Peggy had snapped. "And *don't* call me Peg."

It had been like that from the first moment she'd arrived. Marg had spent days tidying her room, getting rid of all the junk, so there would be space for Peggy's clothes in the drawers and the closet. She'd put fresh sheets on both beds, so that Peggy could choose if she'd rather sleep close to the window or by the door. And she'd neatly arranged her precious collection of dolls on the shelf.

When Peggy had arrived, she looked around and said, "Dolls, what a baby!" And then, "What a poky little room. Am I supposed to share it with *you*?" She'd opened the closet door, looked inside and added, "So where's my bathroom?" And when Marg had explained that, though there *was* a powder room downstairs, basically they all had to line up for the upstairs bathroom, Peggy had sighed heavily, emptied her cases out on the bed and said, "Here, you can hang these up. I hope you've got padded hangers." Which Marg hadn't, so the gorgeous dresses had to go on ordinary wire hangers, and the piles of underwear and designer shorts and tops were crammed in the two drawers that Marg had made ready for her.

Meanwhile, Peggy had wandered over to the window and looked at the view of the ravine and the big tree which shaded the house so beautifully in the summer. She'd sighed again, twitched her long hair over her shoulders and begun to brush it. Marg had looked up at her enviously.

"What are you staring at?" Peggy had snapped.

"I . . . I wish I had pierced ears too," she'd found herself stammering. "But Mom won't let me."

"I had *mine* done years ago."

Then Mom had called them to dinner and Peggy had swept downstairs, looking cool and elegant, with Marg puffing along after her.

"Peggy, you look lovely. And what an attractive dress."

Marg had wanted to say that Peggy hadn't lifted a finger with her unpacking and there'd been no time to clean up before dinner, but Mom had turned to Peggy and said, "I do hope you'll be comfortable, dear. Let me know if there's anything you want."

And had Peggy complained about the one bathroom and the poky bedroom, and the wire hangers? No, she'd smiled sweetly and said, "Everything's just great, thank you, Aunt Jess."

It had been like that ever since. Lovey-dovey to Mom and Dad and rotten to her. When Hairy Harry slobbered all over her in front of them she patted him and said, "Good dog," but when they were alone she said, "Get that gross dog out of my way. He smells."

Harry doesn't smell. Well, only a bit if he gets his fur wet. I really have tried to be friends, though I don't think Mom and Dad believe me. I think they like her better than me; she's beautiful and slim and smart, everything I'm not. Mom keeps saying, "You can't be trying." And "Try a little harder, Marg." They don't understand that she simply doesn't want to be friends. When we're alone she just ignores me. When Mom's around she puts on a look that makes Mom think I've been beating up on her or something. I hate her. But today's my birthday, and she can't spoil that.

Quietly Marg slid out of bed and dressed in shorts and T-shirt, keeping an eye on the lump in the other bed. It didn't stir. She tiptoed out of the room and downstairs.

"Hello, birthday girl!" Mom and Dad got up from the breakfast table to hug her. The kitchen was full of sunshine and there was a pitcher of orange juice on the checkered tablecloth. Mom poured batter into the waffle-maker. Marg looked around the room. Life was absolutely perfect.

"Eight o'clock. I'm off."

"It's a shame you have to work, Dad. You should be here for my party."

"I'd certainly rather do that than drive up to Grande Prairie, chick. It's going to be a cooker of a day. Think of me melting away on the highway. I'll be back the day after tomorrow." After he'd kissed Mom he gave her an extra hug. She felt his smooth cheek and smelled the clean scent of his aftershave.

After he'd left, Marg felt depressed, just for a second; but then Mom put slices of bacon and the first golden waffle on her plate, and she concentrated on buttering it and trickling a careful pattern of maple syrup over the top.

Upstairs the shower ran. It went on and on. "You always tell *me* not to waste water."

"I know." Mom's smile was guilty. "But she *is* our guest."

"She always leaves her towels on the floor and she doesn't dry the walls of the shower stall."

"I suppose she's used to having someone pick up after her."

"Oh, Mom, why do you always make excuses for her?"

It wasn't exactly a quarrel, but it darkened the glory of the special day a bit. Marg ate one more waffle than she really needed, sort of as a consolation.

"Happy birthday, little cousin." Peggy appeared, cool looking in a smart cotton sundress. She put a small parcel down on the table. Marg ripped off the paper, trying to ignore the "little cousin" jab. Inside the small box was a tiny pair of studs. Her crossness evaporated.

"Peggy! Wow! Neat-o!"

"They're your birthstone—rubies. Well, not real. Just pretend."

"They're gorgeous. Thank you. Now I'm going to *have* to have my ears pierced, aren't I, Mom?"

"I suppose you are." Mom's expression hovered between vexation and amusement.

There were two presents from Mom and Dad. The first contained plastic rollerblades, fluorescent pink and green. In the second were matching knee and elbow pads. "And just you make sure you always wear your bike helmet too," Mom warned.

"I will, I will. Oh, Mom, thanks a zillion times. I'm going to try them out right now. Coming to watch me, Peggy?" Marg grabbed her helmet from the hall closet and ran out the door. She strapped on the blades and wobbled down the driveway onto the sidewalk. "Wild. Fantastic!" She looked around to see if Peggy was watching. There was no one there. She pretended it didn't matter and skated gingerly around the block.

That afternoon Marg's best friends arrived for the party, and as she introduced them to "My cousin Peggy from Toronto," Peggy nodded and said, "How do you do? How are you?" in the kind of grown-up voice that made them all feel shy and uneasy. She had put on a fancy black dress with white daisies on it and looked like something out of a fashion magazine, and she didn't want to talk about the things they were interested in or play any of the board games Marg suggested. But then Mom produced fried chicken and pizza and ice cream and pop and cake, and they watched the video of *Beetlejuice*, and it was more relaxed.

"Thanks for the party, Mom. Thanks a lot." Marg hugged her mother as the door shut behind her friends. She saw an odd expression flash across Peggy's face, almost like envy.

"One more surprise for you. A package came special delivery, while you were watching the movie. It's from your grandmother Pargeter."

The package was flat and cardboardy. "Like a calendar." Marg shook it. "But Gran would never send me a calendar."

"And hardly in July! She always manages to find something out of the ordinary, doesn't she? I think she haunts antique shops for lovely surprises for all her family and friends."

"Last year it was a real Victorian doll," Marg said to Peggy. "With a velvet dress and hand-tucked petticoat and panties. I wonder . . ." She ripped off the paper. "Oh, look. It's Victorian, too, isn't it? Look at the printing and the colours. But what is it?"

"Let's see." Peggy seemed drawn to it in spite of herself. "Why, it's a cardboard dollhouse, ready to be cut out and glued together. Look at the picture on the front."

"Oh yes. There's the front wall with ivy climbing up the stone facing. And when you turn the page there's the inside of the house. Look, there's the kitchen down below and the drawing room upstairs and a dear little nursery at the top."

"The blue bits must be the roofs. There's a long one and a square one, and that cone shape must be a tall thin roof like a turret." For the first time that day Peggy seemed interested.

"It looks very complicated, Marg. Do you think you can put it together by yourself? There don't seem to be any directions. Perhaps Peggy would like to help you."

Oh, Mom. "I'm sure I can manage," Marg said out loud. *It's my birthday present*, she thought. *I want to do it my way.* Quickly she closed the covers on the twelve pages of walls, floors, roofs and furniture, and held the book against her chest. *She shan't share it. I won't let her.*

A strange feeling shivered through her body, like the stirring of a dark creature. Something out of a nightmare. To shake off the feeling she said loudly, "I know just what I'm going to do. I'll take it over to the Paper Model Museum and ask Mrs. Makepeace about it. She'll show me exactly how it should be put together."

"What a good idea. If you can bear to wait till Saturday I'll drive you over and drop you off at the museum while I go to the farmers' market. The market's a lovely place, Peggy, with stalls of fresh produce, homemade sausages, baked goods and all sorts of crafts. And wandering musicians. It's great fun. You might like to help me shop while Marg talks to Mrs. Makepeace."

"Thank you, Aunt Jess. I think I'd rather go to the museum with Marg."

"That's settled then." Mom got to her feet with a sigh. "It's been quite a day, hasn't it? Load the dishwasher, will you, Peggy, while Marg tidies up her gifts and I put away the leftovers? Not that there's much. You girls ate like locusts!"

"Just good healthy appetites, Mom. Don't complain." Marg began to smooth out the wrappings to put in the recycling gift box in the basement. As she straightened one piece a small envelope fell to the floor. "Goodness, a card. I nearly missed it."

It was Gran's, and it wasn't a regular birthday card, but a picture of a wistful clown puppet. The inside was covered with Gran's tiny writing. "Oh dear. I can never make it out. It's so spiky and odd."

"Let me see." Mom wiped her hands and took the card from Marg.

Happy twelfth birthday, dear grandchild. Twelve is a very special year, just on the brink of growing up, but still able to look back to the wonder and imagination of being small and believing in magic. It needs to be marked by a very special remembrance. This dollhouse is quite old. It was designed and printed about 1900. I can't imagine why it was never cut out and assembled. Perhaps it has been waiting all this time for Margaret Pargeter to make it come alive. I found it at an antique dealer's in Victoria who knows of my interest in this kind of thing and who saved it for me. He told me a curious story about it, which may be true, or may not—antique dealers enjoy telling "curious stories" to enhance the interest in their wares. He told me that it came in a package wrapped and sealed with wax, with a warning written on the outside. Perhaps "warning" is too severe a word, I don't know. At any rate it said: *Be careful to make this house with love.*

"Oh, I will. I love it already. I'll take terrific care not to spoil it."

"I wonder if that's what the warning means. 'Be careful'. 'Make it with love'. How curious."

"What else could it mean, Mom?"

"Perhaps that you should take care *how* you make it."

"Isn't that what Gran's letter says?"

"Not just taking care. But that love should be a part of the making. Nonsense, really. It's only a cardboard model. As your grandmother Pargeter said, the dealer was probably just making it more interesting."

"I can't wait to show it to Mrs. Makepeace on Saturday."

*   *   *

"It's a lovely piece of work." Mrs. Makepeace turned over the pages slowly. "Museum quality. And I believe I recognize the designer. If I'm right, he didn't make many dollhouses—which increases their value, of course. I must look it up. I suppose you wouldn't consider selling it to me, would you, Marg? You could buy another model and still have a lot of money to put in the bank."

"I couldn't possibly. It's a present from my Gran."

"Oh, well. Of course. That makes it special, doesn't it?" Mrs. Makepeace nodded and put a gnarled hand over Marg's. "But you *will* be very careful how you assemble it, won't you?"

"Funny, that's just what Gran said. . . ."

"You see, just a slip of the scissors or your knife would *ruin* it. As I said, it's museum quality."

"I'll be really careful, I promise. That's why I came today. To show you the house and ask your advice. You see, there aren't any directions."

"Originally it must have been packaged in an envelope, with the directions on a separate sheet inside." Mrs. Makepeace cleared a space on the table next to her cash register in the tiny crowded store that was the smallest room in the house full of paper models. She turned over the pages carefully and pencilled in instructions on the white card surrounding the pieces of model. "You see, this square part of the house comes first, dear. Once it's completely finished you make the other wing, and then the two are glued together and you can put on the turret in the corner."

"That's not too difficult. I'm sure I can do that."

"You must have really sharp scissors for cutting around the main outlines and an X-acto knife for details and small inside angles. And a ruler with a metal edge. Do you see the places where the walls bend at right angles? You have to lay your ruler on the right side and carefully—oh, really carefully, my dear—run your knife along the line of the ruler. You must cut just deeply enough to break through the top layer and no further. Then bend the card carefully so that you get a clean angle. If you have to make an inside angle you do the same thing on the *wrong* side of the piece."

"I don't see why you'd have an *inside* bend. All the walls go round the ordinary way."

"To make the windows and doors, dear. You cut around the opening with your knife, hard, so the knife goes clear through—and, my goodness, make sure you have a board or a thick magazine underneath or you'll mark the table and your mother will be furious! Then you mark the hinge side lightly on the wrong side, so the doors and windows will open outwards."

Marg thought about it. "Yeah, I think I get it."

"You're quite sure you don't want to sell?"

Marg shook her head, her lips pressed tightly together.

Mrs. Makepeace sighed. "I hate to see such a beautiful piece go out of my hands," she said frankly. "Well, all I can say, my dear, is go slowly. Fold the pieces together and try it out before you start gluing. Then glue each piece and hold it steady with your fingers or tweezers—you'll need those for the tiny bits, like the furniture and that turret roof—until it's really set."

"Tweezers. I don't have those, Mrs. Makepeace."

"Eyebrow tweezers would do, wouldn't they?" Peggy spoke from behind Marg's shoulder and Marg jumped. She hadn't seen her come back from looking at the models in the museum. "I'll lend you my eyebrow tweezers—maybe."

"That's great. Thanks." Marg's eyes were on the dollhouse, and she didn't notice Peggy's tone of voice when she said "maybe." "I've got white glue and scissors and a ruler with a metal edge. So I guess all I need is an X-acto knife, Mrs. Makepeace."

"Yes, dear." Mrs. Makepeace dropped the knife into a plastic bag, gave Marg her change and picked up the dollhouse book once more. "That's funny." She shivered. "I thought the clouds had come up just then. But the sky's as clear as clear, isn't it?"

"Yes, it's a gorgeous day. Thank you, Mrs. Makepeace."

As Marg picked up the plastic bag and the book, Mrs. Makepeace put her hand over hers. Her old eyes stared into Marg's. Bright, like shiny black stones. "Be careful," she said. Marg's mouth dropped open. She couldn't take her eyes away from the old woman's. "Be careful," she whispered again.

The sound of a car horn outside broke the spell. "Thank you, Mrs. Makepeace," Marg gasped, pulling her hand away. "That's Mom waiting. We have to go now. Goodbye."

The two girls ran out into the hot sunshine, leaving the old woman standing in the shadowed doorway, her hands locked together. She was still standing there when Mom pulled away from the curb and headed north.

"That's one weird lady."

"She's all right, Peggy." Marg defended her. "We've known her for years. I guess she was just upset about something today."

"Did you get all the information you needed, chick?"

"Yes, thank you, Mom. And Peggy got to see all the models in the museum while Mrs. Makepeace and I were talking."

"Amazing, aren't they? The Eiffel Tower is quite extraordinary. What did you think of them, Peggy? Which was your favourite?"

"They were all very well done," was all Peggy would say. It was as though she hadn't really been paying attention when she was in the museum, Marg thought. As though her mind had been on something else.

They had lunch in Marg's favourite restaurant and she pigged out, as usual. Halfway through she started thinking that it was no good envying Peggy's figure if she never did anything about it. She put her fork down. But on the other hand, not eating her carrot cake wasn't going to help her kinky hair become smooth like Peggy's or her skin become like a cosmetic advertisement. She picked up her fork again. Peggy fanned herself and looked impatient.

It certainly *was* getting hot. They could see thunder clouds piling up in the northwest like the parapets of a castle. When they got home Mom put the sprinkler out on the lawn and they lay in the shade of the patio, too full and lazy to do anything.

Dad came home from his two days up north, his shirt soaking wet where it had been against the plastic of the car seat. He waved at them silently, went into the house to shower and change, and joined them on the patio with a frosted beer in his hand.

He lit the barbecue and collapsed into a chair. "That's more like it. There should be a law against working Saturdays in July."

"Mother and Father often work all weekend," Peggy said. There wasn't anything offensive about the way she said it, but Marg felt that underneath Peggy was criticising Dad and their whole way of life.

She suddenly found herself looking at her family through Peggy's eyes. The small stucco house. The cedar patio that Dad had made himself. The dandelions in the lawn—they were awful this year. Mom in her old sundress, her upper arms and chest freckled, her hair untidy, blue veins showing in her bare legs. Dad with a bit of a paunch showing over the belt of his shorts, his hairy chest—it really was very hairy.

Is this the way Peggy sees us? she wondered and looked across at her. Peggy hadn't changed out of the white dress with the black belt that she'd worn to the museum and lunch. She was wearing sunglasses, so Marg couldn't really even guess what she *was* thinking, but she felt sure that Peggy was comparing them unfavourably with all her posh Rosedale friends.

Her eyes went back to Mom and Dad. They're certainly not the smartest people in the world, she told herself. But they're mine and I do love them. Really. Only perhaps I could get Mom to buy a new sundress and throw out that old one. And maybe suggest to Dad that he wear a T-shirt outdoors. Sometime. Not now.

The clouds were piling higher and higher, and the air was still and sticky. They had hardly finished their hamburgers and fruit jello when the first ominous drum rolls of thunder echoed across the sky. The boughs stirred and the trees suddenly bent over, turning their leaves inside out to show their silvery underneaths.

"This is going to be a corker." Dad hurried to put the cover on the barbecue while Marg folded their lawn chairs and stacked them in the corner of the patio where they wouldn't blow away.

The rain came suddenly, like steel rods shattering white against the road and foaming in torrents down the gutters. The lightning flashed on and off, blue-white, like a laser show, and the thunder shook the whole house. Harry whined and slunk under the dining-room table and stayed there, with his nose under his paws.

It was still pouring when they went to bed. Marg propped up the dollhouse book on her desk. Whenever the lightning flashed, the picture of the house jumped out of the darkness and became real. It's more like a castle, Marg thought sleepily. The Castle Tourmandyne. That's what it's called. When she closed her eyes she could imagine the windows open, lights shining out, the stiff paper dolls moving about inside. *Make me*, it seemed to call to her. *Make me*.

"Tomorrow," she whispered. "Tomorrow I'll begin, and you'll all have a home."

The thunder faded into the distance, though the room was still occasionally lit up by a flash of blue-white. In the other bed Peggy lay still and straight, staring bleakly past the dollhouse into the darkness beyond, listening to Marg's even breathing.

Nearly two months still to go, she thought. Then back to Toronto. And will that be any better? At least at home I have my own room. I can do what I want. No one's fussing over me, asking if I'm having a good time, if my hamburger's just right. All that stuff. As if it mattered. Nothing matters. No one cares if I live or die. If I didn't exist Mother and Father could do exactly what they wanted without having to think about me.

She suddenly saw herself, like a cardboard cut-out of a girl. Looked at straight on she might seem like a normal fourteen-year-old. But if you turned the cut-out sideways the figure would just disappear. Become invisible. Non-existent. That's what should happen to her.

She stared at the ceiling. The lightning flashed again and lit the dollhouse.

TWO

The quarrel started at breakfast next morning. The storm had gone, but in its place was a grey sky and a steady downpour. "It doesn't matter. I'm going to make my dollhouse today. It's a perfect opportunity."

"It'll take you a lot longer than a *day*," Peggy put in with an irritating know-it-all smile. "That is, if you're going to do it properly. Do you know, Aunt Jess, that woman at the museum said it was very valuable—a museum piece, she said."

"Mrs. Makepeace? Really?"

"She wanted Marg to sell it to her for a great deal of money."

"She never said how much, Peggy. And I wouldn't anyway."

"You *will* be careful assembling it, won't you, Marg? It would be such a shame to spoil it. I wonder—maybe Peggy could help you with the difficult bits."

"I can do it, Mom. Goodness, I'm not a child!" Marg felt her face getting hot and prickly.

"And she has to use an X-acto knife, Aunt Jess. Like a razor blade, you know, in a handle. *Very sharp.*"

"I *do* know what an X-acto knife is, Peggy. Oh, dear, I wonder . . . I mean you *are* sometimes a bit of a klutz, aren't you, chick? Wouldn't it be better if you did the main cutting out and left the tricky bits that need the knife to Peggy? That way you could both have fun. Together."

Marg couldn't miss Mom's tone or the pleading look on her face, but she wouldn't give way. It wasn't *fair*. It was *her* birthday present. "Honestly, Mom, you'd think I was still a kid, not twelve years old. I can do it by myself."

"Has three days made such a difference, chick?"

Mom's teasing wouldn't have mattered if Peggy hadn't laughed. She could feel her cheeks get hot. "It's my dollhouse, not Peggy's. And I'm going to make it myself, so there!" She pushed back her chair so it scraped horribly on the tile floor and thumped upstairs, slamming the bedroom door after her.

The dollhouse book stood where she had left it, half open, so she could see the picture on the front: a three-storeyed ell-shaped house with a big stone porch almost filling the inside corner of the ell, little balconies with painted ivy climbing up to them, dormer windows set into the blue-slated roof, the turret and stonework steps up the edge of the sloping roof. *Make me*, it said again. *Open my windows and doors. Make me real.*

She picked it up and began to turn the pages. There was a mother and father, a girl skipping rope, a dog rather like Hairy Harry. And a young man with a soft brown moustache, romantic looking. *Free us from the pages*, they seemed to say. *Give us life.*

I will. I will, she promised, hugging the book against her chest. And stupid old Peggy won't interfere.

There was a tap on the door and Mom poked her head around the edge. "May I come in?"

"I suppose so." Marg could feel herself blushing. She knew that Mom thought she'd been pretty silly. But I won't give in, she promised herself. I just won't.

"There are two things to consider, love," Mom said quietly, sitting down on Marg's unmade bed. "The first is simply the matter of being kind and thoughtful to your cousin, who's a guest in our house."

"I sure never asked her to come," Marg muttered, but Mom went on as if she hadn't heard.

"Then there's the possibility of spoiling a beautiful and apparently unique gift just because you might not be skilful enough to do it well—not to mention cutting yourself on that knife."

"Oh, Mom, as if I would! I'll be careful. And I love my dollhouse. I wouldn't hurt it for anything."

"I'm sure you wouldn't mean to, but accidents *do* happen. Chick, I can't believe that you're letting a little thing like this become a major problem."

Marg couldn't think of any useful arguments, so she stood silently facing her mother, her face flushed and prickly, her arms folded over the dollhouse book.

"I can't understand why you've got this attitude," Mom went on. "Peggy's a lovely girl, intelligent and friendly, with such beautiful manners."

"I bet you'd rather she was your daughter than me," Marg muttered.

"Don't be ridiculous. Honestly, Marg, sometimes I have no patience with you . . . But that's got *nothing* whatever to do with what we're talking about, my girl, so don't try and put me off. If you insist on being selfish and obstinate, then I'm afraid I'm going to have to give you an ultimatum. Either you let Peggy help you or I'll confiscate the dollhouse and not give it back until I'm sure you're old enough to put it together properly and safely."

"You can't do that, Mom. That's not fair."

"There's no law that says mothers have to be fair. I'm just making what seems to me to be the best decision—and it's your obstinacy that's pushed me this far."

"I'll . . . I'll phone Gran and tell her what you've done," she threatened.

"Go right ahead. And I'll talk to her too. I can't think what she was about, giving you a museum piece. But of course, she wasn't to know that you were still so childish. Though she *did* warn you to take care."

Marg wasn't listening. *Make me*, the doll-house clamoured. *Make us come alive*, pleaded the mother and father, the skipping child, the young man. To allow Gran's gift to be hidden away in a closet for years and years was unthinkable. She sighed.

"Okay, she can help. But you've got to tell her to play fair, Mom. Remember, it *is* my birthday present."

"I'm sure she will—"

"Well, I'm not. She's real sneaky and mean when you're not around, Mom. Tell her I get to do everything except the difficult bits, okay?"

"All right. Now, for goodness' sake stop fussing about it and come downstairs and make friends with Peggy and finish your breakfast."

Mom made them make up and shake hands, which Marg could tell Peggy thought was pretty silly. Her cool fingers barely touched Marg's hand. But she did promise to play fair.

After they'd tidied the bedroom and brushed their teeth, Marg carefully unfastened the stitched pages from the cover and used her scissors to cut along the outline of the four walls that made up the left wing of the house. There was a base, made like the lid of a cardboard box, around which the wall, scored and bent at right angles, had to be wrapped and glued.

That's when the trouble started. "I can't wait to see it all come together. Hurry up, Peggy, and finish scoring the walls so I can stick them together."

Peggy put her hand over the cardboard. "That's just what I meant when I spoke to Aunt Jess. You're in far too much of a hurry. Left to yourself I bet you'd have the whole thing put together in five minutes, and all botched up."

"It wouldn't be."

"It would too. I have to cut around the windows and doors first. *And* score the hinge side so they'll open and close. You can't do that once it's all assembled. It has to be flat."

"But you're so slow. I want—"

"Look, why don't you start cutting out the furniture and the dolls. That'll keep you busy for a while."

"That's not fair. Mom said you had to share, Peggy. It's *my* birthday present. I'm supposed to—"

"Hush up, or I'll tell Aunt Jess you're being mean to me."

"She won't believe you."

"Oh yes she will. I know just how to tell her. Then you'll be in bad trouble and she'll take away the dollhouse altogether. Want to risk it?"

Her lips curled into a sarcastic smile and Marg's hands doubled up into fists. Then she sighed and put down the glue bottle. Fighting just wasn't worth the hassle. Peggy would make a big fuss and *she'd* get into trouble. She began to cut out the cardboard people. Like the walls of the house, their figures were printed on both sides of the cardboard, so they had a front and back view. A half-moon of cardboard extended beneath their feet. When it was split and bent, and glued to another circle of cardboard, each figure stood securely upright.

The skipping girl wore a full rose-coloured dress with a hem halfway down her calves. She had high socks and little black boots that laced up over her ankles. Her hair was long like Peggy's and hung straight down her back. Marg tried to imagine herself as the pretty skipping figure, but she couldn't. She sighed and set the figure upright.

"See, Peggy, she looks just like you . . . Hey, that's not fair. You went ahead and glued the walls. You were supposed to let me do that, you know you were."

"It has to be done exactly right or else nothing else will fit properly. You'd just have messed it up."

"I would not!" Anger boiled up inside her. "You are so mean!"

Peggy wasn't even listening. "It looks great, doesn't it?"

Marg had to admit that it did. The leaded casements were pushed open, so that you could see inside. The kitchen had a stove painted on the far wall, and a battery of pots and pans hung on the left, next to the window, which had a geranium on the sill. Upstairs was a grand-looking room with a fireplace. Paintings in elaborate gold frames hung on the flower-striped walls, and there was a circular carpet in the middle of the floor. All it lacked was the furniture. At the top of the house, tucked under the eaves, was a small room that must be the nursery, since it had a wallpaper of toy soldiers marching around it.

"I'm going to do the roof of this section of the house now," Peggy announced challengingly.

"No, I want to do that." Marg tried to grab the page, but Peggy snatched it away.

"It's far too complicated for *you*. The cornices have to be scored and folded and fastened at the top for the roof to rest on."

"What's a cornice?"

"See? You wouldn't even begin to know how to do it, would you?"

"I could if you showed me."

"These strips have to be folded into long thin triangular shapes, then they're fastened to the tops of the walls and the roof's glued to them."

"It doesn't look that difficult."

"Actually it's quite tricky. Get out of the light, will you?" Peggy gave her an irritatingly smug smile and bent over the desk, knife and ruler in hand.

I hate you, Marg said silently. She had picked up the skipping girl and was turning her in her fingers, not really noticing what she was doing. *You're so mean. I wish . . . oh, I just wish . . .* But she couldn't think of anything horrid enough for cousin Peggy.

She carefully set the cardboard figure down and began to cut out the other inhabitants of the dollhouse. The mother was dressed in dark blue silk, tucked and embroidered across the front and around the hem of the skirt, which touched the floor, straight down over her tummy in front, and full at the back. She had a wide belt around her tiny waist and her hair was bunched up on top of her head. She seemed to Marg to have a distant, unfriendly expression on her cardboard face.

"This is the Castle Tourmandyne," Marg muttered to herself. "So you must be Lady Tourmandyne. You're a mean person. You hate your daughter. No, she isn't your daughter. She's your niece. Most of the time you shut her up in the nursery at the top of the house. Her name's Celine. Poor Celine. Look at you skipping rope outside. Just wait till Lady Tourmandyne catches you! You'll be sorry. It'll be bed without any supper for you."

"What on earth are you muttering about?" asked Peggy, as Marg finished the figure and glued it to its round base. "You sound totally nuts."

"None of your beeswax, nosey," snapped Marg. "As for you, Sir Basil Tourmandyne," she went on to herself, her scissors snipping around the outline of the next figure. "You look very grand in your army uniform with the breeches and high boots and those gold epaulets on your jacket, but at heart you're a miserable coward. You go along with everything Lady Tourmandyne does, even when you know it's wrong. Like keeping poor little Celine prisoner."

"You can hold this piece of the dormer window, if you like," Peggy said, as if she were offering her a special treat. "Just till it dries. I want to make sure the roof's secure."

Marg picked up the skipping Celine and transferred her to the attic nursery. "There. You can stay there. Serves you right."

She took the piece Peggy was holding out to her, a tiled dormer with a stone-faced window glued to its front. "You haven't made this window open."

"Of course not, stupid. It's just stuck to the roof. It doesn't really go through to a room behind. It's pretend."

"Well. I'm going to imagine it's real. There's a tiny room up there, and you get to it by the staircase inside the tower there."

"There isn't a staircase inside the tower, dummy. It's pretend too."

"Not in *my* castle, it isn't. You can get to the tower from Celine's room too, and the stair goes down to the next floor."

"You're really nuts." Peggy laughed. "You can hand me that dormer now. I'll glue it onto the roof. There. That's all we can do for now. It needs to set."

We, thought Marg bitterly. *Much chance I've had to do any of it*. "I'm going to go ahead and cut out another person," she said defiantly. "There's just one more besides the servants. And the dog." She began to snip around the outline of the tall man with the brown hair and droopy moustache. He was dressed in a tweed jacket and pants.

When he was finished and standing upright on his cardboard circle, she looked at him critically. "Now, who are you? I don't think you're family. You're Celine's tutor, that's who. She's *far* too rich to go to school and have fun. I wonder if you're a friend? Or maybe you're on Lady Tourmandyne's side and you're mean to Celine too. I bet that's it."

She wondered what his name was. Jones and Brown were too commonplace. Montague was too pompous. It was funny. The names of the other characters had just jumped into her head as if they were already named. But this character eluded her. She'd have to wait.

"Don't worry," she told him. "I'll find out who you are."

Then Mom's voice called up the stairs that it was lunchtime, and she had to follow Peggy down.

"Just a salad," Mom apologized. "It's too muggy for anything else." She mopped her face with a tissue. "I don't remember a summer as oppressive as this. You'd think the rain would have cooled things down. I suppose you're used to this kind of humidity in Toronto, Peggy."

"I don't know how you stand it all the time. It's only like this for a week at the most out here," Marg put in.

"We *do* have air-conditioning, of course."

"Oh dear, yes. I suppose so. Poor Peggy, you must have found it very warm upstairs. How is the dollhouse coming, Marg?"

It seemed to Marg that her mother looked at her sharply as she asked the innocent question. On her lips hovered the response: "I wouldn't know. I don't get to do anything." But she changed her mind at the last second and shrugged. "All right, I guess."

There was an awkward silence. Marg noticed that Peggy got a little pink and then laughed and said quickly, "Marg's busy naming all the dolls and giving them a life story."

But they're not dolls, Marg thought. They're like images of real people. And it's not a dollhouse. Not really. It's a model of a grown-up house, a real house.

"Oh, Marg's got a great imagination," Mom was saying to Peggy, as though they were two grown-ups talking together and she was just an invisible child. It wasn't fair. Why should the gap between twelve and fourteen be so huge?

Perhaps Mom could feel the tension, because she packed them into the car after lunch and took them to the swimming pool. Marg cheered up. She loved swimming, but when she saw Peggy—slim and straight in a gorgeous magenta swimsuit—raising a critical eyebrow at her rather too tight suit, she was miserable again. I do look like a blimp, she thought, as they showered and went to the pool. Peggy dived in and swam in a perfect crawl to the far end.

"Look at that," Mom said admiringly. "What a form. I wonder if she could give you some hints."

"Forget it, Mom." Marg jumped into another lane and began to swim splashily along, wishing that she'd never met Peggy. If Peggy wasn't here she'd be having fun with her friends right now, but there was no way she was going to inflict her snobby cousin on them again. The birthday party had been bad enough.

Back home she slumped down in front of the television set and ignored Peggy. They went to bed in silence, each keeping strictly to her own side of the room and not saying a word, even when Mom came in to kiss them goodnight. It's horrid having to share a room with an enemy, thought Marg, lying in the darkening room watching the dormer window curtains billow softly to and fro. I can't feel comfortable and relax. It's like when I had the measles, prickly all over.

Never go to sleep on your anger, Mom had said once. But surely it wasn't *her* place to make it up with Peggy. It was Peggy who was being mean. Anyway, she had tried lots of times and Peggy'd just snubbed her, hadn't she? Making out she was just a little kid. But she couldn't say her prayers, the way she did every night before she went to sleep, because of the bit about "as we forgive those who trespass against us." So she tried to pretend that prayers didn't matter anyway. She turned on her side away from the window, shut her eyes tightly and began to imagine Celine's life in the castle with Sir Basil and Lady Tourmandyne.

Poor Celine. All alone in her attic bedroom, with no loving father or kind mother to come upstairs and kiss her goodnight, she thought, knowing somehow that Lady Tourmandyne would *never* climb the extra flight of stairs to say goodnight to her niece. Poor, poor Celine.

Peggy lay in the other bed watching the curtains move back and forth. She wondered what her father and mother were doing right then. Perhaps they would be dancing to the orchestra of some flashy hotel in Bangkok, their eyes always on each other as they danced, the way they always were when they were together; romantic, under a tropical moon. But of course in Thailand it was quite a different time of day. She tried to puzzle out which way the ten hours' difference in time went, but got muddled—did you add or subtract the extra hours? Maybe it was morning and they were bargaining in a noisy Thai market for carved furniture or silks.

Whatever time of day or night it was, she knew that they'd be together, the way they liked to be, sharing a secret life that excluded her. They never wanted me. They'd be happier if I'd never been born, she thought.

"You've got Marg. Talk to her. She'll understand," a small voice inside her protested, but she brushed it aside. Marg wouldn't, couldn't possibly understand. Anyway, she'd ruined any chance of being friends with Marg, just as she had with Felicity and Candice back at school in Rosedale. Just the way she seemed to spoil everything, even though she didn't mean to.

Her stomach knotted and she felt sad and empty inside. She stared at the billowing curtains until her eyelids finally closed. . . .

When she opened her eyes again she found that she was standing in the middle of the bedroom, facing one of the dormer windows. Only someone had closed it, so the drapes were unmoving. What was she doing? Sleepwalking?

She'd better get back to bed before Marg woke up and saw her standing here like an idiot.

But when she tried to move she found she couldn't budge. Not a muscle. It was as if she were rooted to the floor. She looked down and saw her feet, not bare as she had expected, but covered in ugly old-fashioned black boots with laces up over her ankles. Above the boots were white socks that came up to her knees, which in turn were hidden by the hem of a full-skirted pink dress.

Oh, it's just a dream, that's all, she thought with a surge of relief. She stood, having no choice in the matter, and wondered what was going to happen next. That was the way dreams worked, wasn't it? One found oneself in a place that was at the same time both strange and oddly familiar, as if one had been there before, had visited from time to time in other dreams, forgotten until the next dream. But in dreams one either left—opened a door and went through into another part of the dream—or else the world itself changed into something else, or a new person came into the dream.

Peggy waited for one of these things to happen. She went on waiting. She was not exactly tired in spite of standing motionless for so long; in fact her body felt—insofar as it felt anything—that *this* was the position it was used to. Just standing, staring towards the window. Time passed. She had no way of measuring exactly how much time. She began to be bored. Surely something must happen soon?

A slow terror began to creep over her like frost. Suppose this wasn't a dream after all? Suppose some magic had transported her to this unreal, unmoving world where she was to be stuck for ever and ever, never waking up? Suppose she had gone mad? It could happen, couldn't it?

She was staring unblinkingly ahead of her all the time these terrifying thoughts tumbled through her head. Directly in front of her a row of toy soldiers marched stiffly across the wallpaper. They had red jackets and blue trousers and black busbies on their heads, and each of them carried a toy musket over his shoulder. Like her, they seemed to be going nowhere.

How long had she been standing here? Was it nearly morning? Staring at the window directly in front of her, she could see nothing through the small, unfamiliar panes but a deep and impenetrable blackness. It didn't change. It hadn't changed in all the time she had been here. She was suddenly thankful that the window *was* closed. If it were open the blackness, which seemed to her so real as to be almost solid, might come trickling in over the sill like black tar, slowly filling the whole room, until there was no air left to breathe.

If only she could look around. If only she could comfort herself with the thought that, even though she was trapped here in this never-ending, never-changing dream, behind her were the two ordinary beds and in one of them Marg was comfortingly, ordinarily asleep. Even as she dwelt on this possibility, she *knew* that it wasn't so. That behind her was an empty room and outside the closed window was an empty world.

The terror was so enormous that she felt her heart jump in her chest. She gave a great gasp that was almost a groan. She heard the sound, the first since she had found herself rooted to the floor of this strange room. Then she felt her bare toes curl against the comforting rug. In front of her she could see the oblong of the window, the curtains moving like ghosts. Behind them she could see a greenish transparent light at the bottom of the sky. She could hear the sleepy dawn chorus of birds nesting in the ravine.

Was she able to turn around? She was almost afraid to try. She forced her body to move and *there* were the two beds. She could see the whiteness of the one whose covers had been thrown back. In the other a lumpy shape stirred and muttered.

She leapt across the space to the empty bed and pulled the covers up around her shoulders. She was shaking with cold and she rubbed her feet against each other and wrapped her arms over her chest, hugging her shoulders with her hands. After a time, warmth began to flow through her body again and she began to relax. Her eyes closed. She forced them open again and stared at the oblong light of the window.

I can't go to sleep again, she thought. Suppose the dream comes back? I can't face it. She lay on her back, her hands clenched at her sides, the nails biting into her palms. Then she got up and sat on the window seat, waiting for morning to come.

THREE

Marg woke slowly and stretched luxuriously. Another gorgeous day of summer holidays. Mom's making pancakes for breakfast, I can smell them. Yummy. What'll I do today?

Entertain Peggy, that's what. The glory of another perfect summer day was sucked away as if by an invisible vacuum cleaner, leaving nothing behind but the prospect of boredom, and the knowledge of hours of bickering ahead, bickering for which *she* would get the blame.

She remembered, guiltily, that she'd gone to sleep last night without saying her prayers, still mad at Peggy. I *will* try today, she promised herself. Whatever she wants to do I'll go along with, however boring. She opened her eyes, glowing with good resolutions, and the first thing she saw was the figure of Peggy slumped on the window seat.

"What on *earth* are you doing over there?" The question slipped out without her stopping to think.

Peggy jumped, sat upright and turned stiffly to look at her. "Nothing. Just looking at the view."

"But you were asleep. Weird. Why'd you want to go to sleep on the window seat?"

"I was *not* asleep."

"You were too. I saw you."

"You're just a stupid little girl. You don't know anything. I'm going to take a shower." Before Marg could think of a thing to say her cousin had sprung up and slammed out the door.

Stupid little girl! Gee! Marg got up and stumbled angrily downstairs to the powder room on the main floor. No use waiting for Peggy. She always took forever in the shower. The whole holidays were being ruined. As if to match her mood, she found, when she got upstairs again, that the inviting morning sun was now obscured by clouds. Before she'd finished dressing there was a rumble of thunder and the rain began to come down in torrents. As she passed the bathroom door on her way downstairs again she could still hear the shower running in competition with the rain outside.

She picked up the hall phone and dialled. "Joy? Hi, it's me, Marg. How's it going? . . . Well, that's just it. It's a pain. I've *got* to escape. I was wondering what *you* were doing today. . . . Yeah, I see. Well, have fun. Talk to you later."

She dialled again. And again. It seemed that fate had conspired to trap her in the house with *her*. Every one of her friends was either already out or had plans for the day.

"Marg, is that you?"

"Yes, Mom."

"Come and eat your breakfast. Whatever you're doing can wait till later."

Marg sighed, dropped the phone back in its cradle with a crash and stomped into the kitchen.

"What a grumpy face. What can have gone wrong so early in the morning?" Mom dished up a pile of pancakes and put them in front of her.

"Peggy, of course. I really do try, Mom, honestly. But she started off by calling me a stupid child and then hogging the bathroom. Mom, do I *have* to entertain her all the time? I'd like once in a while to go out with my friends." She slathered on butter and poured maple syrup lavishly over the pile of pancakes.

"Why can't you invite Peggy to join in whatever you girls want to do?"

"Oh, Mom! You saw what she was like at my birthday party. A real drag. She just about ruined the whole day!"

Mom ran her hand through her hair and

leaned back against the kitchen sink, looking at her. "I wish you could try to be more tolerant, love. You really seem to be prejudiced against her."

"I'm not, Mom. It's *her*."

Mom sighed. "Suppose I take you out somewhere. Where would you like to go?"

"What's the point, Mom? She'll hate everything."

"Don't be so negative, and *don't* talk with your mouth full. We have to try . . . why, good morning, Peggy. I hope you slept well?"

"Good morning, Aunt Jess. Thank you, yes."

"Pancakes?"

"Thanks, Aunt Jess. Just a couple."

"The rain's not going to last," she said, pouring orange juice. "I think it'd be fun to go to Fort Edmonton Park today. It'd be a shame for you to go home without seeing it, Peggy. You'll find it very interesting. The city's rescued a lot of historic buildings that would otherwise have been demolished, and set them up in the park in chronological order. A kind of time travel, starting with the reconstruction of the old fort."

"Like Upper Canada Village, I suppose." Peggy sipped her orange juice, apparently unimpressed. "Only smaller."

"Quite different actually, since it reflects settlement in the west rather than in Upper Canada. You'll enjoy it."

"Yes, Aunt Jess." Marg noticed that Peggy sounded almost meek.

* * *

At least getting out of the house gets me away from the memory of whatever happened last night, thought Peggy, as she followed Aunt Jess and Marg around the old fort. She could almost imagine voyageurs pulling their boats in to the landing and walking up the slope to the fort. Though the trees were pretty scrawny compared with the giants that had been cut to make the beams across the basement ceiling of Rowand House.

But then, as the clouds rolled away, the sun grew hotter and hotter, and she felt the familiar feeling of boredom, like a grey blanket, settle over her. Marg bounced from place to place, going into every house and store on 1885 Street. "Haven't you been here before?" Peggy asked her, as Marg stared raptly at the merchandise on display in the general store.

"Oh, sure. Lots of times. But I love imagining what it'd be like to live back then, dressed like her, for instance." She pointed at a woman walking down the dusty boardwalk in a long dress fitted tight at the waist and high at the throat. She chuckled. "She reminds me of Lady Tourmandyne."

"Who's that, dear?" Aunt Jess asked.

"No one special," Marg said.

"Marg's crazy imaginings," said Peggy at the same time. But when they got to Rutherford House, the house of the first premier of the

Province of Alberta, and Marg exclaimed, "It's furnished just like my dollhouse," Peggy had to agree.

It gave her a very odd feeling to go upstairs and peek into the bedrooms with their flowery wallpaper, almost as if she were in another world. She found herself stopping at the top of the stairs. Shouldn't there be another stair leading up to the nursery? To a little room and a tower. She found herself standing with a hand against the panelling. But there wasn't a third floor, stupid! She went quickly downstairs and sat on the bench outside until the others came out.

"You look quite pale," Aunt Jess exclaimed. "You shouldn't be sitting in the sun like this. Come on. We've seen quite enough. Let's go home now."

She put her arm quite casually through Peggy's. She couldn't have known, thought Peggy, that she was feeling so dizzy that she could hardly walk straight by herself. What had happened to her inside Rutherford House? It was almost as though she had been momentarily pulled back into the past. Yet it hadn't felt like Edmonton's past, but someplace quite different.

It was a relief to get home. Aunt Jess had closed the windows and drapes and it was almost cool inside. Her head began to clear after a long glass of cool lemonade.

"Are you all right, Peggy?"

"Yes, thank you, Aunt Jess. But I believe I'll go upstairs and lie down for a bit, if you don't mind."

"Of course, dear. We won't disturb you."

It was hotter upstairs and Peggy almost turned back. But she needed to be alone. And there was something else . . . something drawing her upstairs.

As soon as she opened the bedroom door she knew what it was. The partly completed dollhouse stood on Marg's desk, just a tall, thin tower of stone-edged brick, its blue-tiled roof broken by the single dormer window. It looked unfinished and forlorn, out of proportion, seeming to call out for the other wing of the house to be added to it.

Peggy sat down at the desk and her hands reached automatically for the scissors. She began to cut out the foundation, a shallow ell-shaped box that fitted into the corner of the tower. Then four outer walls and an inner one to separate the rooms. Floors. It went together smoothly, perfectly. She reached again for the glue.

"You rotten cheat! You liar! Telling Mom you wanted to rest! That's *my* birthday present. You've got no right to . . ."

Peggy jumped violently and the bottle of glue fell over. She hadn't even heard Marg come into the room. She looked at the walls of the dollhouse standing in front of her, almost complete. Had she really done all that?

She could feel the colour rise in her face, and her heart began to race. She had no memory of putting it all together. *Was* she really going crazy?

"Well?" Marg accused.

She was going to have to say something. She couldn't tell the truth, that the dollhouse had called to her to finish it, that she had done all this work in a kind of trance, not really knowing what she was doing. She decided to bluff it out and managed a laugh.

"It wasn't a lie. More of a social excuse. You wouldn't have wanted me to tell Aunt Jess that the whole day was a dead bore, would you? And that I couldn't wait to get away from you all for a bit?"

She saw Marg's face flame, and for a minute she thought she'd gone too far, that Marg would actually attack her. But, though Marg's hands curled into fists and she took a step forward, she did nothing more. She stood silently for a minute and then turned and went out of the room.

Peggy looked at the nearly completed dollhouse and shame flooded over her. What a rotten thing to have done. And then to make it worse by being insulting. Why *had* she done it? She got to her feet, ready to run downstairs and apologize. But, as she glanced at the half-finished house, it seemed to call her back. There's still the roof to do, she found herself thinking. And the main porch and balcony, and the little turret to be completed . . .

Her hands groped for the scissors and she began to cut out the turret. It was painted to resemble the "stone" that faced the corners of the house and the windows. It had eight sides and a high pointed roof, like a church spire, and two windows, no more than slits really, one looking out at the front of the house, the other along the line of blue slates that tiled the roof.

I wish I had a room like this, she thought, as she cut into the narrow corners with the X-acto knife. A room of my own with no one to bother me. A tower away from the whole world. Carefully she began to score along the lines that, when bent, would shape the tower roof into a cone with a tip as fine as the point of a newly sharpened pencil. She bent the cardboard and glued the join, holding the completed piece in the tweezers. It was nearly finished.

"Peggy!"

She flinched and nearly dropped the tower roof. That was Aunt Jess's voice. She was probably coming upstairs to bawl her out for being mean to cousin Marg. Oh well. She shrugged and pretended to herself that it didn't matter. That nothing mattered.

"Peggy," Aunt Jess called again. "Supper time!"

So cousin Marg hadn't snitched on her. Somehow that made the shame of finishing the dollhouse without her even worse. How was she going to face her accusing eyes across the dinner table?

"Peggy!" Aunt Jess was obviously getting impatient.

"Coming." She got reluctantly to her feet, put the roof down—it was dry now—and went slowly downstairs. It was hard to believe that the whole afternoon had slipped by. How hot it was! She felt quite sick and shaky, as if the house had drawn the life right out of her.

They were all out on the patio. She could see them through the sliding screen door, the picture of the perfect happy family. Uncle Greg had come home. He was laughing at something and ruffling Marg's hair. Aunt Jess looked up from tossing the salad and smiled at the two of them.

Too much, another of these folksy barbecues, Peggy said to herself, pushing down the pain that had risen up inside her chest at the sight of the three of them together. They didn't need *her*. They didn't *want* her. She took a deep breath, slid open the screen and went out to join them.

"Hi, everyone!" Even to her own ears her voice sounded false. They turned and for an instant she saw, reflected in the expressions on their faces, the way she looked to them. I forgot to change, she realized. I didn't do my face, I didn't put on any blush. I probably look like death warmed over. How could I have forgotten?

"Sorry," she said into the silence. "I must have fallen asleep. Did I keep you waiting?"

The excuse came so easily, as if that was what had really happened, that it was only in Marg's expression that she recognized it for what it was: a lie.

"Never mind. Nothing's spoiled. Help yourself to potatoes and salad, relish, whatever. Come and sit by me. I've hardly seen anything of you, I'm afraid."

"Thank you, Uncle Greg. That'll be lovely. What a feast! Aunt Jess, how *do* you expect us to eat all this after the lunch we had at Fort Edmonton Park." She began to describe, in hilarious detail, all the food on the menu at Jasper House Hotel, the hostelry on 1885 Street. But nobody else seemed to find her description funny, and her voice trailed off into an embarrassed silence.

Uncle Greg took her plate and loaded it with grilled sausages. She caught Marg's eye and smiled, but Marg looked bleakly back at her as if she were invisible. *It's my fault*, she told herself. What a fool I am. *She'd have been a good friend if I hadn't ruined it all.*

Uncle Greg and Aunt Jess kept the conversation going, though they must have noticed that neither she nor Marg had much to say for themselves. At last the meal was over and the dishwasher loaded; but then there was the long slow evening to get through, the sun still unnaturally high in the sky.

"Why don't you girls go to the show at the planetarium?" Aunt Jess suggested.

With *her*, thought Peggy. She looked quickly at Marg, but Marg wouldn't look back or say anything. It would be horrible if they were made to go and had to sit side by side and walk home, still in total unforgiving silence.

"I'll tell you what . . . why don't we all go?" Uncle Greg's cheerful voice broke the awkward silence. "Make it a family outing."

That made it bearable. She could walk with Uncle Greg, while Marg went ahead with Aunt Jess. She ran upstairs to change into a clean dress, brushed her hair till it shone and put on enough concealer to hide the dark circles under her eyes.

"Quite the elegant young lady," Uncle Greg teased when she came downstairs, and she played up to him and chattered about nothing in particular all the way to the Space and Science Centre.

In the darkened theatre, lying back in a padded reclining chair, she was alone with her thoughts again. The commentary and the background music washed over her. The stars wheeled in precise and geometric patterns across the dome above her head, and the planets whizzed along the path of the ecliptic. It was all marvellously orderly. If only people were as orderly. If only *they* made some sort of sense. She drifted away into a daydream in which her two wonderful parents doted on her, in which she was the most popular girl in school, in which . . .

The night sky faded, the planetarium machine sunk slowly into its resting position in the centre of the room, and the lights came on. She looked around, blinking.

"You weren't asleep, were you?" Uncle Greg joked.

"Of course not. It was far too interesting!" She prayed that he wouldn't quiz her about the show on the way home.

The sun was almost setting, and the brilliant gold and orange sky made the colours of the petunias and geraniums that lined the main walk seem unreal, as if it were all a stage set. In fact there was something unreal about the whole evening. Uncle Greg's and Aunt Jess's voices seemed to come from a long way off and she had to strain to hear what they were saying. Though cousin Marg hadn't said a single word to her, she chatted away to her mother and father.

And I'm on the outside, Peggy thought. No, it's not like that. It's more as if they're on the outside and I'm in a kind of prison, made of glass. I can see them, but I can barely hear them and I can't touch them at all.

Even when they got home and Uncle Greg hugged her, and later on, when Aunt Jess came up to kiss them goodnight, she could barely feel the human contact. I'm a long way off, she thought. And getting farther away.

So she was not entirely surprised when the dream came back, the dream of being alone. She wasn't in the same place, the room with the toy soldiers. This was a much smaller place.

Roundish, with no ceiling, but walls that seemed to vanish into a pencil point of shadow a long way above her head. At least this time I can move, she thought, tilting her head back to look, and felt less frightened.

There seemed to be no windows, but a faint white light permeated the whole space, as though she were inside a pearl, if such a thing were possible. In dreams, I suppose anything's possible, she thought. Then . . . yes, of course this *is* a dream.

She walked slowly around the enclosure, tracing her progress with a hand on the wall. It felt smooth and white, as if white had a certain texture. And the room wasn't round. There were eight walls. It took her several circuits of the room to make sure of this, since each wall was identical to the last. In the end she dropped a handkerchief, which she found in the pocket of her full skirt, and counted walls until she came back to the beginning. Definitely eight walls.

As she picked up the handkerchief she felt that she had won a small victory over some unknown opponent. She was in a small eight-sided room, like a turret. She wondered where the handkerchief had come from? It seemed too real to be part of a dream, and she admired its edges, finished in fine satin stitch, with one corner scalloped into a design of flowers, the petals cut away so that the corner was like lace.

She put it back in the pocket of her old-fashioned cotton skirt, which was of a deep rose-coloured cotton, with a tucked hem that reached halfway down her calves. Below the hem were knee-high socks and black boots with laces that, instead of threading through holes, were laced around shiny black hooks.

She looked around again. She hadn't seen a door, but obviously there must be one. White on white, it would be almost invisible. She walked around again, running her fingers along the smooth walls, feeling for a crack. It was ridiculous. Why would anyone build a room with no door?

It was secret, of course, that was it. She would have to touch exactly the right spot, and then one of the walls would slide aside and she would be released. Again she examined every wall. And again. Until her head was spinning and her legs gave way under her and she collapsed in the middle of the white floor.

Maybe there's a trapdoor, she thought desperately, and crawled over every square centimetre of floor, feeling for the catch. But it was as smooth as the walls.

"Open sesame!" she shouted. Maybe magic worked in this white world. "Abracadabra. Come on, there must be a password."

You'll never find it, a voice inside her said coldly. Or *was* it inside?

No door. No windows. So where was the air

coming from? Perhaps there *was* only a limited supply and when it was used up she would suffocate. The thought made her heart pound. She tried to breathe, deeper and deeper. But in spite of her gasps she was suffocating . . .

"Peggy. Peggy, wake up!"

Gasp. She could feel cool air rush into her lungs. She gasped again and felt her head whirl dizzily. She couldn't stop gasping.

"Here." Something hard and crackling was pushed over her mouth and nose.

Slowly her heart stopped racing and her breathing became normal. She pushed the hand away and sat up. Marg was standing by her bed, tousle-haired and plump in cotton babydoll pyjamas. She had a paper bag in her hand.

"You were hyperventilating. It must have been some dream!"

"Yes, I guess it was." She tried to remember, but already the details were fading. "There was no air. I was trapped and I couldn't breathe."

"Are you all right now?" Marg's voice had suddenly gone stiff and self-conscious, as if she'd just remembered that they hadn't been talking to each other.

Remembering too, her own voice sounded awkward. "I'm fine now. Thanks. How did you know about that trick with the paper bag?"

Marg shrugged. "No big deal. Janet—she's in my grade—she gets hysterical sometimes and starts breathing funny. Mrs. Ferguson always gets her out of it by making her breathe into a paper bag. It's got something to do with the effect of carbon dioxide on the brain."

"I wasn't hysterical," Peggy snapped, as the anger that always seemed to lurk beneath the surface flared up again.

"Well, I know *that*. Are you okay now?"

"Sure. Fine."

"Goodnight then."

"Goodnight."

After Marg had hopped back into her own bed, Peggy lay staring at the faint oblong of light beyond the window. There was something comforting about it. About the occasional creak of the house itself, of Marg's breathing, of the distant hum of the refrigerator and the sleepy sound of birds awakening.

She remembered that in her dream there had been no sound at all. It had been like suddenly being struck deaf, being cut off from all comforting human communication.

FOUR

As soon as Peggy woke up, her eyes turned to the dollhouse. So nearly finished. It wouldn't take long . . . But Aunt Jess was calling them down to breakfast and before she got to the kitchen she could hear Marg begging her mother to take them out to some provincial park. She felt a sudden irrational dismay. *I can't go. I must stay and finish it.*

She hesitated outside the kitchen door. Maybe she could pretend to have a headache. Then the two of them would go to this park place and leave her in peace to get on with finishing the dollhouse.

"Could I bother you for an aspirin?" She managed to get her request in before Marg started talking about the day's plans, so it wouldn't sound like an excuse. Guiltily, she saw the smile fade from her cousin's face.

"Not coming down with anything, I hope?" Aunt Jess's cool hand briefly felt her forehead. "You don't seem to have a fever."

"I'll be fine. Just an aspirin and a little quiet."

"I'll get you one, dear. Then a quiet day in the shade and I expect your headache'll go away. It was very stuffy last night, unusually so. I expect that brought it on."

"But Mom, we were going to picnic at Elk Island," Marg objected.

"Another time, chick. There'll be plenty of opportunities. After all, there's a whole six weeks of holidays left."

It was a perfectly ordinary thing to say, and Peggy knew that Aunt Jess meant it just like that, but, nevertheless, the phrase "six weeks left" seemed to hang in the air like a judgment. Peggy couldn't help noticing the expression on Marg's face. She'd give anything to get rid of me, she thought. I'm just a drag.

She munched her toast and drank a cup of tea in silence. Aunt Jess went outside with a load of laundry to hang out. Peggy couldn't help noticing the sulky expression on Marg's face as she moodily buttered another slice of toast.

"Come on, Marg," she said briskly. "Stop stuffing your face and we'll finish the dollhouse today."

"I thought you were supposed to have a headache?"

For a moment she'd forgotten. "Oh . . . well, the tea's helped. Anyway, today's the exciting day. We put the two halves together and then we can add the front porch, the turret room and the roof. We'll have done it!"

"You mean *you* will," Marg muttered. "You didn't let me do anything interesting, not once."

"But don't you see, this way it'll be perfect, like that woman—Mrs. Makepeace—said: museum quality. You'll actually own a museum quality dollhouse and you'll have it to play with for years and years." Peggy saw Marg flush and she bit her lip. "I didn't mean . . . I know you don't *really* play with dollhouses. Tell you what, once we've finished I'll let you try on all my clothes."

"Really?" Marg brightened. Then her face fell again. "They'll never fit me. I'm too fat."

"Fat?" Aunt Jess had come back into the room. "It's only puppy fat. Though you'd slim down if you didn't eat quite so many sweet things," she went on, looking pointedly at the pile of strawberry jam precariously balanced on top of Marg's toast. "You know, it's just as well we changed our minds about going to Elk Island Park. That's a funny-looking sky out there. I think we may be in for a whopper of a storm later. Off you go, you two. I'm going to do some cooking and then clean out the kitchen while I have a day to myself. Tomorrow's hospital volunteer day and the Art Council board the day after. I've been shamefully lazy this summer. So off you two go and stay out of my hair." It was said with such a nice smile that Peggy realized that it wasn't intended to be insulting.

"Come on, Marg." Peggy ran upstairs.

Finish me, the dollhouse said.

"Yes," said Peggy.

"Yes what?" asked Marg, coming into the room on her heels.

"Yes, let's get going."

Marg squatted down by her desk and looked at the long ell of the house. "I never noticed before. The walls aren't finished on the inside. What a shame!"

"That's only the centre section. The windows there don't open and once the two wings are glued together you won't see that part."

"Why didn't you cut those windows open? You told me it was supposed to be done first."

"Because they're not supposed to open, silly. Look. Both ends of the dollhouse open, so you can put furniture and people inside and play with it, and look through the windows at it. But the centre of the house, well, there's no way in, so there's no point in decorating the rooms. And if you had the windows open in that section you'd *see* it was unfinished."

"Wouldn't it be weird to live in a real house

with a bunch of totally empty rooms in the middle, with windows that wouldn't open? Actually, they're worse than empty, aren't they? They're just a sort of white nothingness, like cloudland. I wonder what it would feel like . . . Hey, what's the matter? Your face has gone all pale. Is your headache worse?"

"No, it's not that. It's nothing." How could she possibly explain the sudden, lurching fear that made her hands and feet sweaty and cold in spite of the warmth of the room? Why had it happened? Why was she so afraid? She took a deep breath and managed to say, "Come on, let's get going."

As soon as her hands were on the two sections of dollhouse, fitting them together, she felt a surge of energy through her body, almost like electricity, and the sense of panic faded. It didn't quite go away, though. She could feel it lurking, like a shadow, in a dark corner of her mind.

"Let me do that." Marg grabbed the bottle of glue.

"No, you'll spoil it. This is the absolutely vital bit. If it's not perfect the roof and the turret won't fit properly. Trust me."

"It's not fair. I'm going to tell Mom."

"Go ahead, sneaky. See if I care. But don't forget she said to keep out of her hair. She won't be too pleased if you go running down like a baby, bothering her about nothing."

She saw Marg flush a deep red and knew she'd gone too far again. But it didn't really seem to matter any more. The only thing that mattered was finishing the dollhouse, making it quite perfect. "Oh, go play with the dolls, why don't you?" she said carelessly.

She went on with her work, going slowly, carefully, though it was a terrible temptation to rush ahead, before the glue was completely dry. She rested, holding the sections together with her hands. They tingled, an electric tingling. Her heart was hammering like mad. Hadn't Aunt Jess said there was likely to be a storm? It certainly felt like it. In the distance, a long way off, she could hear Marg babbling to the dolls.

"Good morning, Lady Tourmandyne. What a frown! Have you been mean to Celine again? I wonder what you're plotting to do with *her*. Something really rotten, I know. *Poor* Celine. Good morning, Sir Basil. How grand you look in your fancy uniform with the gold epaulettes. You're a colonel in the Hussars, I think. You'd be quite nice really, if you were married to someone else. But you're no match for Lady Tourmandyne, are you?"

"You're nuts, d'you know that?" Peggy released her hands and took a steadying breath. Now the front porch—solid stone, with a balcony above—had to fit into the corner between the two wings, and the French doors from the drawing room had to open onto it without scraping on the floor of the balcony. She held her breath and fitted the porch in its place. Perfect.

Marg ignored her and went on muttering to the dolls. "Poor little orphan Celine. Nobody loves you, do they? Left all on your own in the nursery while the fierce guard dog prowls around outside, so you can't even go out and play. Poor little Celine."

Peggy laughed. "Celine's supposed to be you, I suppose?"

"Oh, no." Marg sounded surprised. "She's far too pretty. Look. She's just like you, with long hair down her back. Didn't you notice? Only I call her Celine. 'Celine' seems to fit the castle better than 'Peggy'."

Peggy reached for the glue bottle and began to apply a thin line along the join of porch and house. Her fingers were shaking and she had to stop and take another steadying breath. So the doll was supposed to be *her*? Then why did Marg keep referring to her as "poor little Celine"? Didn't Marg realize that she had *everything*?

"I can't wait to get back to Toronto," she found herself prattling. "I've got so many friends there. And you should see the house. Why, maybe one day *you* can come and visit *me*. I've got a huge bedroom, with its own bathroom, of course, and a walk-in closet. There's a guest wing and a swimming pool and tennis courts. . . ."

She stopped. Marg wasn't impressed. She wasn't even listening.

"There's the cook. She's nice. Fat. I bet she cooks good meals, only poor Celine just gets bread and water. And this is the butler. I don't much like the look of *him*. This maid's got a friendly face, though. I wonder what she's called? Susan sounds right. Now what about you?" Peggy saw her turn over in her hands the figure of the young man in the brown tweed suit. "You look quite nice with your brown hair and your moustache, but you're not. I can just tell. Underneath you're mean and hateful."

Peggy laughed out loud. This kid was spooky. "You sure have a lot of imagination. Who is this character and what's *his* name?"

"I know *who* he is. He's Celine's tutor and he's horribly mean. See that walking stick? Well, it's not *really* a walking stick. It's for beating Celine with if she doesn't do exactly what he says or if she gets her math wrong."

"And his name?"

Marg sighed. "That's a puzzle. It's funny, because naming the others was easy. They just *came*. But he—I dunno. Whatever I think of is wrong. It's as if he already had a name and I had to guess it."

"Like Rumpelstiltskin?" Peggy joked, but Marg nodded.

"That's it exactly. There's power in names, isn't there? Well, I'm sorry, whoever you are, but you'll have to make do with another name until I find out who you really are. I'm going to call you . . . Quentin Harrowpoint."

"What a ridiculous name! What made you think of it?"

"I don't know. It just popped into my head. It's a mean, pointy kind of name. Like him. Yes." She held the figure up. "You're Quentin Harrowpoint and you're evil right through."

"I don't imagine that Celine's parents will put up for long with a tutor like *that*," Peggy joked, playing along. She felt more comfortable now that Marg was in a good mood again. Her hands had stopped trembling and she pushed the porch section into the angle where it belonged and held it tightly in place.

"That's where you're wrong. Sir Basil and Lady Tourmandyne are only interested in going to parties and drinking champagne and stuff like that. Anyway, Celine's just their niece. *Now* they've discovered that Celine will inherit a massive amount of money, enough to build her own castle with bathrooms attached to every room and *two* swimming pools. So—o—o . . ." She drew the word out dramatically.

For some reason it wasn't funny any more. "Oh, this Celine must have *some* friends. Someone who'll help her out of this danger."

"Nope." Marg shook her head. "She's so selfish that there's nobody in the whole world who cares about her. *Poor* Celine."

"You know what? That's a *really* stupid story.

Come over here and hold these two pieces together. Careful. Don't let them slip."

By early afternoon the dollhouse was finished. The turret was in place, its two slit windows gazing blindly out. The big stone porch with the balcony above filled in the corner of the ell between the two wings of the house. The chimneys and dormers were secure.

Marg knelt by her desk so that her eyes were on the same level as the main-floor windows. "It's all so *real*. Look at the ivy climbing up the outside and the flowers around the foundation. And when the windows are open you can see right through the house. I'm going to decide where all the furniture goes. *And* the people."

Her voice challenged Peggy, but Peggy felt no inclination to argue. Her work was done. She felt drained of energy, as if the house had somehow sucked her life force into itself. Which is ridiculous, she told herself. It's only cardboard and glue.

So she sat on her bed and watched from a long way off, as if she were looking through the wrong end of a pair of binoculars, as Marg swung open the end walls of each wing, so that the kitchen, the drawing room and the nursery were exposed at the left side, and the dining room, master bedroom and attic at the other. She watched her begin to arrange the furniture.

"But how are they supposed to get from one

end of the house to the other?" Marg suddenly exclaimed. "There's that boring section that won't open in the middle, getting in the way. But there *are* doors." She peered inside. "Look, there are doors in the kitchen and the drawing room that are supposed to lead through into the middle of the house. And at the other end there's a door in the dining room *and* in the master bedroom. Even in the attic. Oh, I never noticed. There's even a tiny little door in the nursery. It must lead right into the tower that's in the corner there. How spooky!"

Peggy suddenly shivered and rubbed her arms. It was ridiculous to be chilly. The room was stiflingly hot.

"I wish you had cut open those inside doors, Peggy," Marg complained. "If I'd have been making it I'd have made them all open. It'd be much more real."

"But they're not *supposed* to open. That's why the centre section's not finished inside. I explained all that already, stupid."

"Stupid yourself," Marg answered automatically. She didn't move from her knees beside the table. "I wonder what it would be like to open one of those doors and go through to the secret part of the house." She hiphopped the cardboard figure of Celine across the dining room to the panelled wood door on the back wall. "Open sesame!"

It was like her dream all over again. Peggy

jumped to her feet. "That's a really dumb game. Come on. Let's get out of here. It's stifling. Let's go out and find something interesting to do."

"You know, you don't make any sense at all. You're the one who spoiled our plans to picnic at Elk Island Park with your stupid headache. It's a shame. We hardly *ever* get to go, because Mom's got such a lot of volunteer stuff. And I don't believe you even *had* a headache. I think it was just an excuse to get out of the picnic. Now the dollhouse is finished, but, instead of being all excited about it, you don't seem to *care*."

"Okay, so I change my mind a lot. Oh, do come on. Let's get out of the house. I'm sure there's going to be a storm. I feel prickly all over."

"Really? Or are you telling lies again? I hope there *is* a storm. I love lightning, don't you? Zapping across the sky, and the thunder like all the percussion in the orchestra at once. *Bam!*"

"You would." Peggy turned her back on the child and walked out of the room, which now held a strange terror.

"Good riddance," muttered Marg once she was alone. "It's my dollhouse and I can do just what I want with it." She took the cardboard furniture out of the rooms and, with the point of the X-acto knife, began to saw carefully around the edge of the dining-room door, the one that led into the mysterious centre of the house.

Now that the panels were no longer flat, she

wasn't able to score along the hinge side and make the door open properly, the way Peggy had done with the other doors and windows. But when she pushed her finger against the door it *did* open slightly, enough to show her the darkness that lay beyond. She hopped the doll Celine across the dining-room floor and pushed her through. The door snapped shut behind her.

"Oops! Poor Celine!" Marg giggled and tried to open the door far enough to get her out again, but she could only put one finger through and, though she could touch the cardboard figure, she couldn't catch hold of her. Tweezers, that's what I need, she thought.

But Mom called just then. "Want some lemonade, chick?"

"Thanks, Mom. I'll be right down." Oh well, Celine, I guess you'll just have to stay there for now, she thought. She put back the furniture carefully in the rooms and set the servants in the kitchen and Sir Basil and Lady Tourmandyne and the horrible Quentin Harrowpoint in the drawing room.

Mom and Peggy were on lawn chairs on the patio. Peggy was lying back, looking wrung out.

"It must have been like an oven upstairs, Marg. You really shouldn't have kept poor Peggy up there all this time. Surely the dollhouse could have waited?"

Marg opened her mouth and shut it again. What was the point?

Peggy took a sip of lemonade and smiled bravely. "It's all right, Aunt Jess. I'm fine, really."

You are *too* much, thought Marg angrily. You twist everything around so it's all *my* fault, and whatever I say to put it straight is going to make *me* sound mean and disagreeable. She poured herself a glass of lemonade and took a long, cool swig. Then she remembered the Celine doll trapped in the limbo of the inner part of the house and giggled.

"Sorry, Mom. I guess I'm just a slave-driver at heart."

"Just remember not to take advantage of Peggy's good nature, chick, that's all."

Good nature indeed! "Oh, I *will* try, Mom," she said.

Her tone of voice made Peggy open her eyes and stare at her. She stared right back. *I know something you don't*, she gloated.

Was that a flash of fear in Peggy's eyes? She saw her hands tremble. She put down her lemonade and clutched the arms of her lawn chair.

"My goodness, but it's a funny day," Mom said, out of the blue. "Can you feel the electricity in the air? And just look at those clouds. I hope it's not tornado weather."

FIVE

I've been here before, was Peggy's first thought. The place was both totally strange and tantalizingly familiar. A white space. I *have* been in a white space before. I can remember it vaguely, like a dream. A small, round space. Very small.

This, on the contrary, was huge. It was like being inside a great white cathedral. When she looked up, her eyes travelled towards some white and shadowy space that seemed endless. In front of her was white. To left and right, white. A place without boundaries or shape.

She backed up, away from the nothingness of the white, and felt her shoulders touch the comforting reality of a wall. She turned to it. White again. But it was, at least, something she could *feel*. She moved her hands over it, hoping for the outlines of a door, but the wall was as smooth and featureless as the space around her.

It was firm, though. It was real. It and the white floor were the only things she could make sense of. Being surrounded with whiteness was almost like being blind. She would have to rely on touch.

She set out to trace the shape of the space, her left hand on the wall all the time, afraid that if she lost contact she might never find it again. Sooner than she expected, her eyes giving no clue to distance, she bumped into another wall at right angles to the first. She followed it, lost it and had a moment of panic before realizing that she had to turn left again. It was not the real corner, but only a jog in the space. About ten paces later she found the real corner of the room and turned right again. Twelve paces. Right turn. Thirty paces. It was a long room. Fifteen paces. She must be back in the corner where she first started.

Now, although she still could not see it, she knew that she was standing in the corner of a room thirty paces long, with a jutting out piece on the left, so that, though the wall close to her was fifteen paces across, the far wall was only twelve. The shape of her prison.

"There must be doors," she said aloud. "If it's a real place there *have* to be." She tried not to panic.

Her voice didn't echo, as it should in a large high room, but seemed to be absorbed by the whiteness as if it were made of cotton batting. But even white cotton batting rooms must have doors, she told herself again.

Unless I'm crazy, of course.

The thought lurked in the whiteness that surrounded her. The only sounds were the thumping of her heart and her breathing, harsh, as if she'd been running.

Crazy.

She could remember a voice saying, "You're crazy!" But she couldn't remember who it was, or if the voice had indeed been talking about her. But it echoed inside her head. *You're crazy*.

No, I *am not*! I know who I am and where I am; I am standing in a white room, thirty by fifteen paces. I know my name; it's . . . my name is . . .

This is ridiculous. I have to know who I am.

The terror of being nameless was far worse than her initial fear at finding herself in this no-space. She turned back to the end wall and beat her fists against it, sobbing.

"Let me out. Please let me out."

Part of the wall suddenly creaked and moved reluctantly outward against her weight. A line of daylight ran around its edge, instantly transforming the milky white of the place where she had been into darkness. She pushed again, her shoulders to the door, and fell through into a comfortably furnished, amazingly ordinary sun-filled room.

Directly to her right was a marble fireplace, the grate empty except for a fan of pleated paper. On each side stood a chair upholstered in mouse-grey velvet. Around the dining table which occupied the centre of the room were four similar chairs. There was a sideboard against the fireplace wall on the opposite side to the door through which she had just come. A fern drooped its fronds over a stand in the left corner. There were three windows, one in each of the walls except the one with the fireplace. She walked quickly across the room to the nearest window. Her hand was on the wrought-iron handle, ready to push it down and release the catch, when a voice called.

"Celine? Celine, where are you hiding?"

It was a hateful voice, a voice that made her shudder, though she couldn't say why. She drew her hand back from the window and stood still, half concealed by the heavy velvet curtains, her heart pounding. But in spite of the fear, there was also relief. For of course that was her name. *She* was Celine. It was a relief to own a name and a place. For now she also remembered—if it was remembering—that this was where she lived. That this was *her* home.

"Celine! Celine, answer me at once."

The voice was louder, as if the person was close at hand. She cowered against the curtains.

The door by the fireplace burst open with a protesting squeal of its hinges and through it strode a tall, slender, youngish man. She saw that he was dressed in an oddly old-fashioned waisted jacket of brown tweed, and long, narrow trousers that accentuated his height and thinness. His brown hair curled at the nape of his neck and his moustache was soft and luxurious. Below it his lips parted in a far from pleasant smile and his teeth flashed whitely.

"So there you are, Miss. Why did you not obey me when I first called you? And what are you doing in Lady Tourmandyne's dining room? You have no business in this part of the house."

She stared at him dumbly. *Had* she lost her mind? Or her memory? There was a blank, like that moment when she seemed to have forgotten her name. Now she felt that she should know him; that he was, in an odd way, familiar, in the same way that the name, Celine, was familiar as soon as she heard it. But . . .

"Cat got your tongue? Back to the nursery, if you please. It'll be bread and water for you at suppertime for this little escapade."

She clung to the drape with her right hand, feeling the comforting reality of its dense pile under her fingers.

He strode forward and grasped her left wrist in his right hand. It felt cold and unpleasantly damp. Then his left hand came up and she saw, in the instant before it struck, that it held a riding crop.

It was the shock almost more than the pain that made her cry out. She saw the greedy flash in his eyes, the way the moist red lips parted in a smile, and she swore to herself that she would not again give him the satisfaction. When the second blow landed she was ready for it, her lips tightly compressed to hold back any sound.

His own lips tightened. He jerked her arm cruelly, so that she had to move towards him. "Back to the nursery, I told you."

He half threw her across the room, so that she stumbled and had to catch herself by grasping the door knob. She hesitated, terrified at the idea of being sent back to that limbo of whiteness, but he strode across the room and stood over her, the crop raised in his left hand.

She pulled the door open and ran through to the other side, steeling herself to bear the terror of no-space. She stopped and gasped.

Where there had been nothing but whiteness there was now a corridor with a polished floor on which lay a luxurious runner. The panelled walls were lined with oil paintings, the eyes of the portraits staring coldly into the eyes of the portraits on the opposite wall.

She walked between the staring eyes, her feet silent on the carpet. To her right there were doors, but they were all closed. Ahead, to her left, a glassed-in lobby jutted out into the room. She caught a glimpse of a hat rack draped with cloaks, and a huge ugly vase stuffed with umbrellas. Beyond, leaded stained-glass windows flanked what must be the main door. She hesitated, but *he* was close behind her. No time to escape, even if the door were unlocked.

To her right rose a curved staircase, its treads and banister polished like glass. She looked up and saw that a gallery ran around three sides of the upper storey, giving access, she guessed, to the bedrooms and, presumably, the nursery. She crossed the wide hall, a sea of waxed floor with islands of carpets. Beneath the gallery were other doors. A fireplace, sofas.

Now *his* hand was between her shoulder blades, pushing her up the stairs. She hesitated on the landing. Through a door on her left she could hear voices, a man's and a woman's. His, quiet, drawling. Hers, as sharp as a pin. No comfort or rescue there, she felt sure. She saw another door, tucked in the corner of the gallery. She opened it, stepped through and heard it slam behind her. A key turned in the lock. She heard the scraping sound as it was withdrawn. The footsteps moved away. She was alone in the pitch dark.

She took a step forward, her hands stretched out in front of her, and stumbled over something at shin level. Something her hands told her was box-like, covered in some rough fabric.

She put a foot up, shuffled forward and tripped again. Recognition clicked in her mind. In front of her was a circular flight of stairs, covered in rough matting, which twisted upward to the right. Her hands feeling for the next step, she climbed. After a full turn a narrow slit of light outlined a door to her left, while the stair itself climbed onward. She pushed open the door and found herself thankfully in daylight once more.

It was a low-ceilinged, rather poky room with a small dormer window thrust out past the slope of the ceiling to her left. The floor was covered with an ugly linoleum patterned in brown and yellow squares. On it stood a small wooden bed covered with a coarse cotton knitted coverlet, a wardrobe and a low dressing table with two of the drawer pulls missing. A small table held a huge china basin with a pitcher of water in it. A square of yellow soap sat in a matching china dish. Beneath the table was a pail, obviously for slops. Beneath the bed was a china chamber pot. A much-darned cotton towel hung from a rail at the side of the little table.

In a corner of the room was a battered wooden rocking horse, but there were no books, no other toys or dolls, to indicate that this was a children's room. Nothing but a dreary design of toy soldiers marching endlessly around the wallpaper.

Her legs gave way under her and she sat down on the lumpy bed and looked around. The whole room should be familiar to her, shouldn't it, since it was hers? Yet only the wallpaper attracted her. Attracted and puzzled her, as if she'd seen it somewhere before.

I'm Celine, she reminded herself. Celine who? Was it Celine Tourmandyne or Celine Someone-else? Maybe there was a clue somewhere in this sparse room. She got up and began to examine everything in more detail. When she opened the wardrobe door, a mirror showed herself, long hair tied back with a pink bow, a rose-pink dress with a tucked bodice and full skirt, and old-fashioned black boots.

When she moved the reflection moved. She peered closely and saw her own familiar blue eyes staring back at her. But the dress was so weird. And those boots! Black, ugly, with worn pointy toes and laces fastening them halfway up her leg. She pushed the door wide and looked at the clothes hanging within. There was not much, a couple of cotton dresses, like the one she was wearing, and one of stiff dark serge with a sailor-suit collar. On the shelf were a white sunbonnet, a straw hat and a huge tam with a wool pom-pom at its centre. When she tried it on it flopped down almost over her eyes. She found herself smiling at her reflection and wondered why she should find it funny. After all, it must be *hers*.

She tossed the tam back onto the shelf and

turned her attention to the dressing table. The two lower drawers were filled with flannel nightdresses, petticoats that tied around the waist with tape, and long cotton knickers with elastic at the knees. In the small top drawer on the left were neat rolls of cotton socks, black and white. In the right-hand top drawer were a brush and comb, both of which had seen better days, white cotton gloves, a pile of cotton handkerchiefs and a small prayer book.

She picked it up. On the flyleaf, in old-fashioned spiky hand-writing, difficult to read, was the inscription:

> *To Celine*
> *On the occasion of her tenth birthday*
> *Lucinda Tourmandyne*

Infuriatingly, it gave nothing away. Except that, surely, Lady Tourmandyne could *not* be her mother, given such a cold and distant dedication.

She stared at it for a long time before closing the book and returning it to the drawer. There was no other place to look for clues. And nothing to do. Bread and water for supper, *he* had said. Even bread and water would be wonderful, she thought. She felt empty clear through. Her last meal must have been a long time ago.

In order not to think about food, she went over to the window. The small panes were so grimed over with dirt that she could see nothing through them, nothing at all. She tried to open the casement, but it wouldn't budge, even when she shook the catch and pushed as hard as she could.

She was still struggling with it when she heard a sound on the far side of the door. She turned quickly, her hands behind her back, ready to face that man. And his riding crop. But the door was opened by a plump serving girl, dressed in white and blue striped cotton almost hidden under a huge white apron. Her hair was tucked into a big frilly cap, and her pink face was creased in a friendly smile.

"Here's your supper, Miss." A tray was placed on the dressing table. A stemmed wine glass full of water. A fine plate, bordered richly in purple and gold, seemed to mock the single slice of bread it held. "Supper, Miss," the girl said again sympathetically.

I must find out who I really am, and what I'm doing here, she thought. "Don't go," she said quickly, as the girl turned from the dressing table. "My mother. . .? My father. . .?" She hesitated and saw tears in the girl's eyes.

"Oh, Miss, it was so sad losing them. But you mustn't feel too badly. Your aunt and uncle, her ladyship and Sir Basil, they're giving you a good home. You don't have to worry about your future, not like some."

"But I'm treated like a prisoner. And I'm so hungry. It isn't right. I want to talk to Lady Tourmandyne. Will you. . .?"

But the girl backed up against the door, her eyes wide. "Oh, Miss, I can't go talking to the likes of her ladyship. It wouldn't be proper. I'm only the kitchen maid."

"But I need help. Please."

"I might slip a message to him . . . to Mr. Harrowpoint. But that's all."

Harrowpoint. Quentin Harrowpoint. The whole name slipped easily back into her memory. Of *course*. But with the memory, a shiver down her spine. The man with the riding crop. Her tutor.

The girl still stood by the door. "Shall I, Miss?"

She gave a hopeless laugh. "Forget it."

"I beg your pardon, Miss?"

"It's all right. Don't say anything to Mr. Harrowpoint."

"Very well, Miss. Goodnight, Miss."

"Goodnight . . . er . . ." I don't even know *her* name, she thought. It's as if she were a total stranger. Yet she obviously knows me very well. I've lived here for some time, I think. My mother and father are dead, and Sir Basil and Lady Tourmandyne are my guardians. It was like trying to remember a story told long ago. Yes, that was right. Another piece of the puzzle slipped into place.

She listened to the clatter of the maid's steps, to the opening and closing of the door at the foot of the staircase. Then there was silence. Marooned in the nursery at the top of the house, she was as separate from the activity of the rest of the house as if she were in a dungeon.

Though at least this dungeon has windows, even if they won't open. She wondered what would happen when it grew dark. There was no light overhead, no switch on the wall. Not even an old-fashioned lamp or candle. She had better eat her meagre meal and get ready for bed before it became too dark to see.

She ate the bread in very small bites, chewing each mouthful until there was nothing left to chew, and she drank the cold water in small sips. When she had finished and picked up every crumb from the plate with a moistened finger, she still felt hungry but a good deal braver.

She was sitting on the edge of the bed, starting to unfasten her awkward boots, when she heard the voices. At first she couldn't figure out where they were coming from, but then she discovered a grating let into the floor of the nursery. It was probably intended to bring some residual heat from a fireplace downstairs, but it also made it possible to hear what was being said in the room below.

She lay on her stomach on the floor, her head close to the grating. She could see nothing, but voices occasionally floated up, as if the speakers were moving around in the room below—the drawing room, she guessed it must be.

"So much *money*." It was the woman's voice, thin and bitter.

"Not worth fretting about, my dear. Only thing to do, treat her nicely and she'll remember us with gratitude when the time comes."

"Gratitude. Do not speak to me of gratitude, Sir Basil. Why, remember . . ." The voice faded away.

The next thing she heard was an exclamation of horror or dismay. "Good God, my lady, you cannot contemplate anything like that!"

"Of course not. My hands will be clean. But his . . ."

"The tutor's?"

". . . why I hired him. I will be rid of her, Sir Basil. I *will*."

She sat up, her heart pounding. So the secret was out. Her aunt was planning to have her killed so that she would inherit her fortune. And Quentin Harrowpoint was to be her instrument.

I have to get away, she thought desperately. I *have* to. As she sat on the floor she heard a door slam below, and the noise triggered a memory. A sound. Or rather the absence of a sound. She had heard the maid's step on the stairs. She had heard her open and close the door at the bottom of the stairs. But she had *not* heard the sound of the key grating in the lock. A large key, she remembered, and a noisy lock.

A glance at the window showed neither daylight nor dark. I'll go right now, she told herself. Before someone remembers that unlocked door. She got quietly to her feet, tiptoed to the door and eased it open. Beyond was the darkness of the spiral staircase, winding up to a tower. Somehow she knew there was no escape that way. Downwards then, through the unlocked door.

She felt her way carefully, her right hand against the outer wall. One full turn and a bit. She fumbled for the door knob. It *must* be here. Desperately her hands went over the surface, encountering nothing but a slick smoothness. Finally, she put her shoulder against the door and pushed.

It swung outward and she with it. Not onto the remembered gallery with the polished staircase descending to the main floor, but into white, dimensionless space. She screamed and clutched at the doorjamb. She felt it melt under her fingers. She fell and went on falling.

SIX

Marg sat bolt upright in bed. What had wakened her? There was no sound of storm out there. The window curtains moved softly. She could see the difference in the light outside the room compared with the shadows within. It must be almost dawn. There was no sound.

And then, from the next bed. "No, oh no!"

"Peggy, are you sick?"

Another moan.

She jumped out of bed and bent over her cousin. Peggy's eyes were shut, her long hair a dark tangle against the whiteness of the pillow, her head moving from side to side. Marg caught her by the shoulders and shook her. "Wake up, Peggy, wake up."

The eyes that stared back at her were dazed and out of focus. "The stairs . . . I kept falling and falling."

"It was just a dream. Only a dream." Marg folded Peggy's cold hands inside her warm ones.

"Is it morning?"

"Not yet."

"What are you doing here? Does my aunt wish to see me at last?"

"What on earth are you talking about? Mom's sound asleep. Why would she want to see you *now*?"

"I don't know. I only hoped . . ." Her voice died away.

"Hoped for what? You're not making any sense, you know."

Peggy shook her head. In the faint light from the window her eyes looked huge, confused.

"I tell you what, shall I get you a glass of warm milk? Would you like that? It'll help you go back to sleep."

"That would be very nice." Peggy mumbled something about bread and water for supper, which made no sense to Marg. She tiptoed down to the kitchen, got out a pan and began to warm the milk. Waiting for it, she prowled to and fro on her bare feet, biting her nails. Peggy seemed even odder than usual. Should she wake Mom and tell her? But Peggy would be furious. Maybe she'd wait till morning and see how she was then. She put a finger in the milk to test it, poured it into a glass and carried it carefully upstairs.

"Here you are. D'you want me to turn on a light."

"Turn on. . .? No, thank you. This is nice. Thank you." Her voice sounded meeker than Marg had ever heard it before, which itself was enough to worry her. She sat on the edge of the bed, swinging her legs, watching Peggy sip the milk.

"D'you think you could sleep now? It's only half past four."

"What time am I supposed to rise?"

"Why are you talking in that weird way? Anyway, don't be silly. You know it's the holidays. You can sleep as long as you like." Marg yawned and climbed back into bed, leaving Peggy propped up against her pillows, sipping her warm milk. "Goodnight."

"Goodnight." Celine put the unfinished milk down by her bed and slid under the bedclothes. How odd. She was in a nightdress and yet she had no recollection of taking off her clothes. She could remember sitting on the edge of her bed, looking at the crossed laces of her high boots. Then . . . then the dream of falling.

She shivered. It was lucky for her the little maid had heard her and come to wake her up. And the warm milk was comforting. She felt sleepy in spite of everything. If only she could be sure that the dream wouldn't come back. Her eyes flew open and stared resolutely at the ceiling. Then they slowly closed again.

The next day was unbearably hot. Even at breakfast time the sun was blazing and the cumulus, piled up in the northwest in towers and turrets like the wall of a medieval castle, threatened storms.

"I hope it doesn't hail. My poor tomatoes. My zucchini." Aunt Jess looked over to the west. "Those clouds look awful, but they aren't moving. There isn't a breath of wind."

She set the sprinkler on the back lawn before going to the hospital to work in the gift shop, and the girls stretched out in the shade of the patio, a big pitcher of icy lemonade on the table between them.

Peggy stretched lazily, looked around and found herself thinking: How nice this is. How peaceful and ordinary it all looks. Then she thought with surprise: That's funny. I've always hated the ordinariness of this poky house and the boring routine. Yet today I feel different. I even feel differently about Marg.

Nothing much happened until the mail arrived, with two brightly coloured postcards for her of temples overgrown with tropical vines. According to the postmarks, they had been mailed almost a week apart, but their messages were almost identical. *We're having a wonderful time*. Obviously, since she wasn't there to get in the way. *We've made some great buys for the store*. Naturally, they both had the knack of buying cheaply and selling for a great deal, though, as her mother had explained to her once, there *were* the overheads of travel and the rent and taxes on the store to consider. *We miss you and wish you were here*. What a lie! *We hope you're having a great summer*. Huh! *Love, Mother and Father*. Lies and more lies.

She was about to tear the cards in two and toss the pieces to the floor when Marg exclaimed. "What gorgeous pictures. Don't you want to keep them? Wow, look at the flowers on that creeper. And the stamps! They're almost as colourful as the cards. Could I have them, *please*? If you really don't want them, that is."

"I don't care. Sure, go ahead if you want them." Peggy closed her eyes and tried to battle the tears and the anger.

"Are you all right?"

"Sure. Why wouldn't I be?" Peggy deliberately buried herself in the book she'd brought downstairs. It was one of Marg's paperback historic romances, and the story was far too unlikely to get involved in, but it passed the time.

They were still out on the patio when Aunt Jess came back from her morning in the hospital gift shop. She brought out salad and fruit and cottage cheese. "You can just help yourselves."

She didn't seem in the best of tempers. "And Marg, you know I don't like you having snacks in your bedroom, but if you *are* going to have glasses of milk in the night, the least you can do is to bring them downstairs in the morning and rinse them out. In this heat the remains of the milk curdled, of course. Disgusting."

"Mom, I . . ." Marg was staring at Peggy, as if she expected *her* to say something.

"I don't need excuses, my girl."

"Sorry, Mom." Marg frowned at Peggy as she spoke, but her grimace meant nothing to Peggy.

Then she remembered. *A glass of milk.* That had been part of a dream, hadn't it? Something about being imprisoned in an attic nursery by cruel relatives, eating nothing but bread and water. And the maid bringing her a glass of milk after a bad dream. How odd. If the glass of milk was real, how much of the rest was? She shook her head and tried to read, but the dream memory wouldn't go away, though it sounded as silly as this romance of Marg's.

The day crawled by. It seemed to her that Marg and Aunt Jess were polite and careful to her, as though she were a stray visitor they hoped would soon leave.

Perhaps I could. But where would I go? The Toronto house is closed up till *they* get back. And I feel so tired I couldn't manage on my own. So tired. She found that even climbing the stairs made her heart pound and her legs tremble.

Ever since the dollhouse was finished she hadn't felt normal.

Uncle Greg came home for supper. He hadn't been out of town for several days. "It's so hot, nobody's interested in anything but going fishing," he said cheerfully. "You don't look so good, Peggy, my dear. How do you feel?"

"Fine," she managed. "It's just the hot weather."

She saw Marg open her mouth and just knew she was going to talk about her nightmares. "Just fine," she said again firmly, glaring at her cousin.

They stayed up to watch a late movie, while outside the thunder rattled and boomed, but the cooling rain never came and at length they crawled up to the hot bedroom again.

"I'm going to take a cool shower," she told Marg. "Maybe it'll help."

"Don't be all night about it," Marg answered. "I haven't brushed my teeth yet."

But as she walked along the upstairs hall to the bathroom she heard Uncle Greg and Aunt Jess arguing downstairs. This was so unlike them that she found herself leaning over the banisters, eavesdropping.

". . . I don't care, Greg. I'm going to phone Christine."

"She won't thank you for it."

"Too bad. But it's too much responsibility. I believe that child's on the edge of a nervous breakdown. I could just *kill* those two. How heartless, going off like that and leaving her in this state."

"Aren't you exaggerating, Jess?"

"You remarked yourself how poorly she looked."

"Well, yes. A little nervous and run-down. But as she said—the hot weather."

Their voices faded as they walked through to the living room. Then Aunt Jess's voice came loudly from just below where Peggy hung over the rail. "Ten time zones difference," she said over her shoulder to Uncle Greg, who must still be in the living room. "It's almost one in the morning now. I've forgotten which way round it goes. Is it three in the afternoon or eleven in the morning in Thailand?"

"Three *tomorrow* afternoon."

"Oh, Greg, what on earth does *that* matter?"

"Hey, don't snap at me."

"Sorry, sorry. It's just I'm worried. And I guess I'd like you to be a bit more concerned yourself. After all, Terry *is* your brother. Peggy's *your* niece."

"All right. I acknowledge that it's a Pargeter problem. But don't you think you're blowing it up out of size? Suppose you *are* able to get hold of Terry and Christine, which is unlikely, since they're wandering all over Thailand. What then? Are you going to ask them to cut their trip short? They certainly won't be pleased about *that*. And what can *they* do that we can't?"

"Start acting like parents, for a start."

"Oh, for heaven's sake!"

The door at the end of the corridor creaked open and Peggy scrambled to her feet and bolted to the bathroom. She quickly turned on the tap.

Marg tapped on the door. "Aren't you through *yet*?"

"In a minute." Peggy stood, toothbrush in hand, staring at the water running down the drain. It was awful, listening to Uncle Greg and Aunt Jess quarrel. She didn't think they *ever* quarreled. And Mother and Father would be *furious*. They would probably force her to go back to that horrible shrink, the one who'd pried and poked and tried to make her reveal her real feelings about Mother and Father. As if she ever would. Because how could she trust him not to tell them? It was hard enough pretending to love them now. It would be impossible if they ever found out what went on inside her head.

What am I to do? She leaned her head against the cool tiles.

The door handle rattled. "*Peggy!*"

"I'm coming." She looked at the toothbrush in her hand and put it back in the rack. She splashed her face, patted it dry and unlocked the door.

"You don't have to be so impatient."

"Mom and Dad'll be up in a moment and they'll want the bathroom to themselves."

"No, they won't. They . . . they're planning to call Mother and Father. I overheard them." The words blurted out.

"In *Thailand*?" Marg stared. "Wow, that'll cost a fortune, won't it? Why would they want to . . .? Oh, I see." She stopped and looked embarrassed.

"You've been telling on me to Aunt Jess, haven't you?"

"I have not. Hey, let go my arm, you're hurting."

"I don't believe you."

"That's too bad. But it's true. I took the blame for the glass of milk you didn't bother to take downstairs. Well, didn't I?"

Glass of milk. But that had been . . . "That wasn't real. That was part of my dream. It was, wasn't it?" she added uncertainly.

Marg was staring at her. Peggy saw her expression change. "You're tired. Come on, Peg. Time for bed." She put her arm around her waist and urged her towards the bedroom. "Now get into bed and stay put. I'll be back in a jiff."

"You won't tell?" But she'd gone.

Peggy slumped back against her pillows. I *am* tired, she thought. Too tired to fight anymore. A couple of tears trickled down her face and she didn't bother to wipe them away.

Marg came back, smelling of peppermint toothpaste and baby powder, and sat down on Peggy's bed.

"Okay. Now, I know I'm only a kid and you're fourteen and live in a house with air-conditioning and fifteen baths, and you get to go to a private school and all that stuff. I don't care. What's important is that you're making yourself sick and you're upsetting Mom, and I want to know why. What's going on?"

"I don't know. I can't explain."

"What about these dreams you're having? How long have they been going on?"

Peggy thought. "Since . . . since your birthday. About then."

She watched Marg nod thoughtfully, and then all the old anger surged up. "What do you know about it, clever?"

"I know you've been dreaming. And waking up scared to death. And not even knowing you *are* awake. That's weird, I can tell you. Something about the stairs collapsing and you falling. You *do* remember that, don't you?"

"They didn't collapse. They just weren't there. Only whiteness . . ."

Stumbling over the words, as the memory of her nightmares slowly came back, Peggy found herself telling her cousin about her dream life, trapped with hateful adults in a house that sometimes dissolved into whiteness around her, but at other times was so real that she felt that *there* was where she really belonged.

". . . and I wonder. Which is the real world and which the dream one? Oh, Marg, it's so scary."

Marg put her arms around her. At first Peggy felt herself stiffening, but it was hard not to respond to the comfort of her cousin's arms.

"I wonder why it seems so real? Is it your Rosedale house?"

Peggy shook her head. "It's old-fashioned. More like the big house at Fort Edmonton Park."

Marg stared. "At the park? I remember, you were looking for another door, a door that led up to the attic. Only there wasn't one. And your face got funny and you said how hot it was and bolted outside. Did that have something to do with your dreams?"

"I could just see a nursery with toy soldiers marching around the walls." She stopped and stared at Marg. "*That* was the dream nursery. With toy soldiers on the wallpaper."

Marg stared back.

"Settle down, girls." Aunt Jess was at the door. "It's very late. Time your light was out. It's cooler now. You should be able to sleep all right." She kissed them both and snapped off the light. "Goodnight, my dears."

"I wonder if she made that phone call." Marg's voice came through the darkness.

"If she hasn't yet, she will."

"Never mind. It'll be all right, Peg. Try not to worry."

"Thanks. Goodnight." She didn't even feel up to snapping at Marg for calling her "Peg."

                        *   *   *

Marg stared at the ceiling, her mind racing, sleep the farthest thing from her mind. She went over the details of Peggy's dream. A nursery with toy soldiers marching around the walls. That was *her* world. *Her* imaginings. How could it possibly have got into Peggy's dreams?

She sat up cautiously and looked across the dark room at Peggy's bed. She seemed to be asleep. She got quietly out of bed and padded over to her desk. Her fingers groped through the drawer and closed around the small flashlight.

She eased open the left wall of the dollhouse and switched on the flashlight. Only a firefly spark of light, enough to show her the nursery and confirm what she already knew in her heart. Red jacketed and blue trousered, with their high black fur hats, muskets over their shoulders, toy soldiers marched across the cream-coloured wallpaper.

Coincidence? Peggy might not consciously remember the wallpaper in the dollhouse nursery, but it was *she* who had cut it out, scored the bends in the walls and glued it together. Her subconscious mind would have remembered that, and remembered the story she, Marg, had made up about Sir Basil and Lady Tourmandyne and the wicked what's-his-name? . . . Quentin Harrowpoint. Peggy could have heard all that and turned it into dream. She remembered telling her that the Celine doll was just like Peggy, really *was* Peggy . . . she could have remembered that too.

Her spark of light travelled through the doll-house rooms, making them spookily come to life, one by one. There were Sir Basil, Lady Tourmandyne and the horrible tutor in the drawing room directly beneath the nursery. There were the three servants in the kitchen below. There was the dog, so like Hairy Harry, mounting guard on the front steps. But where was Celine?

Marg remembered that she had cut a door through to the centre of the house and dropped Celine through. Then Mom had called and she'd left her there and gone downstairs, leaving the Celine doll trapped in the terrifying no-space behind the dining room door. *I did that. I made Peggy's dream happen.*

So maybe I can make it un-happen. If I can get Celine out, maybe right out of the house, then Peggy won't have nightmares anymore. She put the flashlight away and felt for the tabs that opened the other end of the house. Pushing the furniture carelessly aside, she pried the door open with her fingernails and felt in the space behind.

Nothing. She tilted the whole dollhouse and heard the cardboard furniture rattle and slide. She tilted the house again and hooked the cardboard doll through. Let's hope Peggy doesn't dream of earthquakes now, she thought.

Wouldn't *that* be terrible. She shivered and quickly closed both ends of the dollhouse.

Then she held up the doll in her hands, with its long hair and rose-coloured dress, the skipping rope forever in its hands. "You're not really Peggy," she whispered aloud. "You never were Peggy. You're Celine and you're an ordinary happy kid like me, with ordinary parents like Mom and Dad. And there isn't anybody called Quentin Harrowpoint." Was there anything else she should do to undo whatever she had done? "I'm going to put you here on the front steps, Celine. You're free to go anywhere. To do anything you want."

She crept back into bed. If it *was* magic, then she'd made it right again. But if Peggy was just dreaming about the dollhouse out of her own head, then there wasn't anything she could do to stop it.

In the other bed Peggy turned over. "What're you doing, Marg?" Her voice was slurred with sleep.

"Nothing. Goodnight."

Celine stretched in her small, hard bed. The last thing she remembered was the little maid bringing her a glass of warm milk. That was kind. She hoped that she wouldn't get into trouble for doing that. Now the room was light. It must be morning, though when she peered through the windows she could still see nothing.

She washed in cold water from the jug, put on her pink dress and laced up her cumbersome boots. Was the door at the foot of the stairs locked again? She went quietly down the spiral staircase, feeling the roughness of the stone against her outstretched fingers.

At the bottom her fingers felt the door knob. She turned and pushed and the door swung outwards. She hesitated, her heart pounding. Something horrible had happened once before when she'd done this, only she couldn't remember what. Today everything seemed perfectly normal. The light from the stained-glass windows lit the gallery and the polished wood of the stairs with lozenges of colour. The house was silent, tranquil, elegant. There seemed to be nobody about. It must still be very early.

She tiptoed down the stairs, holding tightly to the banister, and scurried across the polished floor of the hall to the lobby doors. They too stood open. She could hardly believe her luck. The lobby was dark, except for the coloured light that filtered through the criss-cross pattern of its leaded windows. The handle to the front door was a great iron ring. It took both hands to turn it, but then the door swung easily inward.

A greyish light. Foggy perhaps. Was fog normal in the early mornings? There were two steps. The door swung shut behind her. She was free. But free to do what? To go where? The whiteness seemed to stretch in every direction, around and above her. It didn't seem to be like an ordinary morning mist, but more as if the house alone existed, as if beyond it was . . . nothingness.

She put out one foot and it vanished into the whiteness as if it no longer existed. Frightened, she ran up the steps again and clung to the door frame. She felt as though, if she didn't hold on to something solid, she would be swallowed up in the mist. But the alternative was to go back into the house. To face *him*. That was more than she could bear.

As she hesitated on the top step, she heard a bark. Then another. Out of the whiteness bounded an enormous dog. Hairy, wide-mouthed. A nightmare beast. She screamed, but no sound came out of her throat. The dog was almost upon her, its forepaws on the step, its hairy muzzle close to her body.

Not daring to turn her back on it, she felt behind her for the door handle. She turned the knob and pushed. The door moved and then stopped, as if someone on the other side were leaning against it.

"Let me in. Please let me in."

Laughter. Hateful spiteful laughter that sent a shiver through her body. "You wanted to get out, didn't you, ungrateful girl? Now you can stay out."

"I'm sorry, Mr. Harrowpoint. Please let me back in."

There was no answer, just more of the humourless laughter.

"Aunt Lucinda. Uncle Basil. Help me!"

"They don't hear you, do they? They can never hear you. There is only you and I, Celine."

Deep in its throat the dog growled. The only possibility of escape seemed to lie in running past the dog into the nothingness beyond the house. But her fear of this was even greater than her horror of the monster dog. If she ran into the mist, she could imagine herself becoming thinner and greyer, until she dissolved and vanished completely and forever.

Desperately she turned her back on the dog and pounded with her fists on the carved panels of the door.

SEVEN

She was pounding her pillow, gasping and flailing her arms around. And cousin Marg was there again, rubbing her back, telling her it was okay.

"Just a dream? Oh, wow!"

"Not the same one?"

"Yeah. Only scarier. He was there again. That's two nights running he's been there." She rolled onto her back and stared at her cousin. "I think I'm going crazy."

"Don't *talk* like that, Peg."

"He wants me dead, d'you know that?"

"Who does? What are you *talking* about?"

"Quentin Harrowpoint."

Marg stared at her, her face flushed and her hair rumpled with sleep, even wilder than usual. "That's garbage. He's not *real*. I invented him, remember? I invented him and Celine and the Tourmandynes. They *can't* harm you. They're only inside my head."

"Well, they're in mine now. And he can. He will." She found herself shivering.

"But I told him . . ." Marg stopped suddenly.

"Told him? What are you talking about?"

Then the whole crazy story came tumbling out, from Marg's first angry inventions as Peggy assembled the dollhouse to the secret cutting of the doorway into the inner part of the house and the loss of the Celine doll inside. "But I made it all right last night," Marg stammered, her face crimson. "I fished Celine out of the middle of the house and put her outside by the front steps. I told her she was free. And I remade the story so that the Tourmandynes were really nice people and Quentin Harrowpoint too."

"It didn't work, did it? You put me outside, all right. With that awful fog and a crazy dog. And *him* inside, laughing and refusing to let me get back." Peggy sat up in bed and stared at her cousin. "Just listen to me! What am I *talking* about? It was a dream. Only an awful dream."

"It's all my fault, Peg. I'm so sorry."

"Don't be stupid. You know, I think we're both crazy, talking seriously about being haunted by a *dollhouse* and a lot of crazy cardboard people. It isn't *logical*." She glared across the room to where the finished dollhouse stood on the desk. "It's only cardboard and glue. And your stories are just—silly stories."

"Then how do you account for your dream of Celine going through the dining-room door to the other part of the house *after* I'd cut open the door and pushed the doll through?"

"Coincidence. Or maybe I noticed what you were doing."

"You couldn't have. You were downstairs with Mom."

They stared at each other. Then Peggy laughed uncertainly. "You're going to try and persuade me that it's really connected? Like magic maybe?"

Marg's face flushed. "I know it sounds crazy. But . . . oh!"

"What is it?"

"I've just remembered Grandmother's letter—the one she sent with the dollhouse."

"So?"

"Something she said . . ." Marg bounced off Peggy's bed and scrabbled through her desk drawer. "Here it is. Let's see . . . Listen. 'I feel it must have been waiting all this time for Margaret Pargeter'— that's me—'to make it come alive. I found it at an antique dealer's . . . it came in a package . . . with a warning written on the outside . . . '*Be careful to make this house with love.*' See?"

She looked up triumphantly from the greeting card.

"No, I don't see. What's that got to do with anything?"

"We *didn't* make the house with love, did we? We made it with hateful anger and quarrelling."

"Speak for yourself."

"Okay, so I was the one who got mad. But Gran did give it to *me*, and she did say she felt it was waiting for *me* to make. And I'd have made it a loving house, Peg, I know I would have. Even if it wouldn't have turned out as neat. But you took it away and made me mad. So I made up that whole stupid story about Quentin Harrowpoint. And you *didn't* make it with love, Peggy, you know you didn't. You haven't been loving to any of us ever since you got here. I think you . . ." She stopped suddenly.

"Go on." Peggy stared up at her cousin.

"Nothing. Forget it."

"You're thinking maybe I don't know how to build a loving house, aren't you? But that's nuts. Loving doesn't come into it. I just concentrated on putting it together perfectly. Every fold line dead straight and crisp. Every glued joint perfect. That's all. Emotions don't come into it. And if you'd have done it, it'd have been a mess."

Marg shook her head. "It wouldn't have been as nice as yours. But I'd have done my darnedest, because it was Gran's gift and she's special to me."

"You don't own her, you know," Peggy snapped back. "She's my grandmother too."

"Oh. I suppose she is. I'd forgotten that. But *I'm* called after her."

"So'm I, silly. Yes, I am. Don't you know that Peggy's short for Margaret too?"

Marg stared. "I didn't know. That should make us close to each other, sharing the same grandmother *and* the same name, almost like sisters."

"I don't see why," said Peggy drily. She swung her legs over the side of the bed.

"Oh, Peggy, don't *do* that all the time!"

"Do what?"

"Smack down a person's love every time it's offered."

"I don't know what you're talking about."

"Yes, you do. You did it with Mom at the airport. My friends at my birthday party. Me all the time you've been here. What are you so scared of, for goodness' sake?"

"Nothing. Why on earth should I be scared?" Her voice shook and she got up and walked quickly over to the window, so that Marg shouldn't see her face. She pulled back the curtain. The sun had risen behind the trees and its light lay in golden tiger stripes across the garden. It must have rained during the night, for a thousand diamond points of blue and crimson sparkled from the tips of the grass. Birds were singing *fee-bee*, *fee-bee* down in the ravine, and a neighbourhood cat slunk belly low towards the hedge. It was all exquisitely beautiful, but none of it was hers. She had no rights here.

She found herself sitting on the window seat, with Marg's arms round her, her head against her cousin's shoulders, shaking with dry sobs.

"You're right, Marg," she said after a while. "I couldn't build that dollhouse with love. I couldn't build anything with love. Not now. The only way I can be myself and not let people hurt me is by being hateful first. It's like . . . oh, you couldn't possibly understand. You're too young."

"No, I'm not. It was like that in grade five. There was a gang of really mean kids that just made our lives miserable. I found out that I could stop minding them if I hated them real hard. Like . . . like a kind of armour."

"You *do* understand."

"I'm not really a dummy, you know, Peg. But the point is it didn't work. I found I couldn't turn the hating off. It got in the way of loving Dad and Mom the way I'd always done. It wasn't worth it, that armour. So I stopped hating them."

"So what happened with the kids?"

"The funny thing was, they didn't bother me any more. I could feel *why* they were the way they were and I could be sorry for them. Then it wasn't so difficult to love them."

"*Love* them? You're nuts."

"That's what we're supposed to do, isn't it? Love our enemies, even if we don't like them very much."

"Oh, you're too much, Marg, you know that?" Peggy found she was laughing as well as crying, and now Marg's arms hugging her felt good, and she was able to hug Marg back. She could feel the hardness inside her begin to melt and for an instant she panicked and drew back. Then she saw the hurt expression on Marg's face.

"I'm sorry. You'll have to be patient. It's been a long time."

There was a knock on the door and Aunt Jess poked her head around the corner. "You're up early, girls."

"Sorry, Mom. Did we disturb you?"

"Not at all. Dad's off for a couple of days up north again and he wants to get an early start while it's still cool. It's going to be a cooker later. Peggy, dear, since you're awake, this might be a good time to talk to you."

Her voice and face were serious and Peggy felt her stomach flip and go tight. "Yes, Aunt Jess."

"Marg, dear, would you mind leaving us alone for a bit?"

"Let her stay, Aunt Jess. Please."

"Are you sure?"

"Yes, really. We're friends now."

"I'm delighted to hear it." Aunt Jess hesitated.

"You phoned Mother and Father, didn't you? I . . . I heard you talking about it last night."

"Yes. It took a bit of doing, but we tracked them down and I talked with them."

"You shouldn't have, Aunt Jess."

"I was worried about you, my dear. You don't look at all well."

"It's just I haven't been sleeping too well, that's all." Peggy managed a laugh and hoped it sounded more convincing to Aunt Jess than it did to her.

"Your mother said you've been seeing a psychiatrist in Toronto."

"They said I had an attitude problem. *Me*. What about them? And he keeps asking me how I feel about Mother and Father!"

"What's wrong with that?"

"Well, he's bound to tell them, isn't he? They're friends. They have secret talks about me, I've heard them. 'How's Peggy? What has she told you? What makes her act this way?'"

"My dear, he's bound ethically *not* to tell them anything you say to him without your permission."

"That's what he said. But you can't trust grown-ups."

"Oh, Peggy!"

"Sorry, Aunt Jess. You're a bit different, maybe. But if he told them just how much . . . just how much I hate them . . . well, they'd never speak to me again."

"You know, Peg, I bet you really *do* love them, otherwise you wouldn't care what the doctor told them," Marg interrupted.

"Hush, Marg. But she's right, isn't she, Peggy?"

"Oh, I don't know. I don't care. It's only *words*, isn't it? I guess what matters is, what did you and Mother decide, Aunt Jess?"

"Your mother's agreed to let our doctor check you over. We'll have to see what he says."

"I won't go to another shrink."

"No. It wouldn't be worth it for the short time you'll be here."

"You mean they're coming back early?" It was hard to keep the happiness out of her voice. Play it cool, Peggy, she told herself.

"No. I'm sorry, my dear. They'll be coming back at the end of August, as they planned. I just meant that there isn't time to establish a relationship of trust with a new psychiatrist."

"They didn't want to come back early? Well, I guess that's good. It costs a lot to fly to Thailand. It'd be a waste to have to cut their trip short, wouldn't it?" she managed to say.

"You *are* a sensible girl, Peggy." Aunt Jess got to her feet, relief on her face. "If you could *just* try to be happy and get on with people."

"I do try."

"I'm sure you do. Don't worry. As soon as his office is open I'll make an appointment with Roger Cummings. You'll like him. He's been our family doctor since Marg was a baby . . ."

"But he's not an old fogy," Marg interrupted. "He's really neat."

Peggy nodded. Her mouth was dry and she couldn't swallow the lump in her chest. She felt as though it was going to choke her. So it was going to happen all over again. Questions and more questions. As if she really knew what she felt.

Dr. Cummings said he could see Peggy that very afternoon, even though he was busy. After Peggy and her mother left, Marg wandered aimlessly around the house. I could go swimming, she thought. Or phone one of the gang, maybe go over there . . . but to do anything like that seemed kind of heartless. She went into the bedroom, her eye drawn immediately to the dollhouse. It had had that effect ever since she'd first unwrapped it. It was commanding. Central.

The cardboard furniture inside was toppled this way and that, as if there'd been a natural disaster in the world of Castle Tourmandyne. She began to straighten out the furniture, and wondered what she could do to take the burden of anger off the house, since freeing Celine and well-wishing the other characters hadn't done a speck of good.

The house is angry because Peggy made it so, not because she's mean, but because she can't help herself. Anger is her only weapon. Like a kind of carousel, going round and round, so as soon as she's asleep she's trapped in the Castle world, living out that anger with those hateful characters . . .

That I invented. The story was my fault. Why did I do it? I've got Mom and Dad and Hairy Harry and all my friends. Why did I grudge

Peggy the dollhouse? If I hadn't invented Lady Tourmandyne and Quentin Harrowpoint, none of this would have happened.

Or maybe it would anyway. *Be careful to make this house with love*. A warning Peggy had ignored.

"Oh, what *can* I do?" she asked out loud, and, quite suddenly, the idea of phoning Granny Pargeter leapt into her mind. Gran lived in Victoria. A long distance call. But I can pay for it out of my allowance. They won't mind if I do that.

She ran downstairs. Gran's number was in the address book in the top drawer of the little desk in the hall. She began to punch in the numbers. 1 . . . 604 . . .

Oh, do let her be in. Please. It had rung eight times and she was almost despairing before she heard Gran's voice, a bit breathless, at the other end.

"Thank goodness you're in, Gran. It's me."

"Marg? My dear child, you sound in quite a state. I was weeding the garden. I usually ignore the phone when I'm outside, but something told me it was important, so I ran. It is, isn't it?"

"Awfully important. Gran, about the dollhouse . . ." The story tumbled out in no particular order, and Gran listened patiently and only interrupted to ask questions when Marg got off track. After she had finished there was a long silence at the other end of the line. Maybe she hadn't explained properly and now Gran thought she was crazy.

"Gran, are you there?"

"Yes, dear, I'm here. I'm thinking. Just a moment. I believe I had better sit down."

"Are you all right, Gran?"

"Yes, thank you. It's just that coming face to face with evil is always a shock."

"You *do* believe me then?"

"Of course I do, child."

"What can I do? It's partly my fault. Maybe mostly my fault. I've tried making new characters, saying they're good and kind. I've tried saying Celine isn't Peggy. But it won't work."

"Of course not. No, it wouldn't, would it? You can't well-wish evil, once you have evoked it. It *is*."

"Then what am I to *do*?"

"You can start by praying."

"*Praying?*"

"Of course, child." The familiar laugh came comfortingly to Marg's ear. "It's the final line of defence against all wickedness, isn't it? *Deliver us from evil.*"

"I never thought of that meaning anything in particular. Just words. All right, Gran. But there must be something I can *do*."

"Be careful. Listen, my dearest child, I mean it. *Be careful.* You're a good girl at heart. You're strong and happy, and there's nothing evil enjoys as much as destroying goodness and strength and happiness. Poor Peggy was easier prey, I expect. All that anger. She's halfway there already. But as for you—*take care*."

"That's what the note on the dollhouse said."

"I know. I didn't take the warning seriously. I didn't think it might mean possible danger to *you*, or I would never have given it to you. Listen, dearest child. I'm going to try and get hold of Mr. Merriman, the antique dealer I bought the dollhouse from. Perhaps he knows something more about its history, something that might help us."

"So we can undo the magic?"

"Perhaps we may. I'll phone you just as soon as I hear anything useful."

"Thank you, Gran. It's so nice talking to you. I'm sorry I made you run to the phone."

"Don't be. I'm thankful I was here. Goodbye, dear child. And remember: pray and be careful."

After she had put the phone down Marg felt as if a weight had been lifted from her shoulders. But the good feeling lasted for only a moment. Upstairs on her desk stood the Castle Tourmandyne, the site of evil, according to Gran.

She shivered. It was spooky being alone with IT. Like a haunted house. But this was not a bricks-and-mortar house. It was only cardboard and glue. What would happen if I tore it apart and burned the pieces? she wondered. No, it probably isn't that easy. The evil would just inhabit somewhere else. At least she knew exactly where it was. Not that that was any comfort.

She looked at her watch. Only two-thirty. Mom and Peggy wouldn't be back for ages and she felt she couldn't spend another minute alone in the house with IT. She grabbed her purse and scribbled a note to Mom:

Gone over to the Model Museum. Back soon. Love.

She ran and caught the bus on the corner and, when she got across to the south side, walked as fast as she could to the museum, hoping that Mrs. Makepeace would be alone, that there wouldn't be a kids' summer camp tour or something distracting like that.

"Why, it's the little girl with the dollhouse. Marg . . .?"

"Marg Pargeter, Mrs. Makepeace. I wanted to talk to you about it."

"Is it finished? Did you run into any trouble?"

"Yes, it's all done. And no, at least not exactly. There wasn't any trouble *building* it. But do you remember you said you were going to see if you could find out who made it? Did you?"

"Why, yes." She hesitated and then went on, reluctantly, it seemed to Marg. "My encyclopedia has several photographs of designs by this artist, very like your particular house. I'm sure it's the same man: Arthur Blair, his name was."

"What did the book say about him?"

"He was a puppet maker first and foremost. Made very realistic puppets. Then he stopped for some reason and turned to dollhouses."

"Yes?"

Mrs. Makepeace was silent, biting her lip. Marg looked at her, puzzled. She was usually very hard to turn off once she started talking.

"Go on," she encouraged. "He turned to dollhouses."

"It seems likely that the dollhouse you own was designed near the end of his life, in 1892."

"How old was he then, I wonder?"

"Only twenty-eight."

"My goodness. So he didn't die of old age then?"

"No."

There it was again. Like a barrier. What was it Mrs. Makepeace was reluctant to talk about? "So what did he die of?" she asked at last, when it became evident that Mrs. Makepeace wasn't going to say another word.

"What a lot of questions you do ask, child!"

"That's because you're not giving me any answers. Please, Mrs. Makepeace, it's important. I'm not just being idly curious, honestly."

"Oh, dear." Mrs. Makepeace got up from her desk in the little gift shop and walked restlessly to and fro, automatically threading her way between the stacks of gift boxes and display shelves. "I'm afraid it's not very nice," she said at last. "According to my encyclopedia, the poor young man ended his own life, quite abruptly, when he was twenty-nine."

"He *killed* himself?" Marg shivered.

"There now, it's upset you. I knew it would. That's why I wanted to say nothing about it."

"I'm not really upset, and it's terribly important to know exactly what happened. Does the book say why he did it?"

"Apparently his mind was disturbed. He left a rambling note about some unknown peril. And then he went and hanged himself. Such a terrible thing to do. Only a dozen or so of the dollhouses he had last designed had been sold at the time of his death, and his executor arranged that those that had not been sold should be destroyed. The book doesn't say why. But that's what makes your dollhouse, still uncut and unassembled as it was, such a rare find. Worth even more than I imagined when I first asked you to sell it to me."

"I wish I had done. I wish I had."

"I'm afraid it isn't worth quite as much assembled as in mint condition. But it would still be worth a good deal of money. If you mean that, I'm sure I could find a buyer. If you really want to get rid of it."

Get rid of it. That's what it would be, wouldn't it? Like passing the hot potato on to someone else, someone innocent and unsuspecting. Reluctantly, she shook her head. "No, I mustn't. It wouldn't be right."

Mrs. Makepeace sighed. "I remember. It was a gift from your granny, wasn't it?"

"That's right. So that's all you can tell me

about him—about Arthur Blair—is it, Mrs. Makepeace?"

And that was it. Marg walked slowly to the bus stop, and the right bus came along almost at once, which never seemed to happen when she was in a hurry to get home. Today she was in *no* hurry at all.

The closer she got to home the more the feeling of reluctance grew. When she was almost a block away it was like a barrier, a barrier made of fear. She could hardly bear the idea of going into the house. The patio was hot, and a sudden wind slammed all the lawn chairs over, so that they collapsed like card houses and skidded across the cedar deck, which made her jump.

By the time she'd picked them up and stacked them out of the way at the corner of the house, the wind was whipping up the dirt, filling her eyes with stinging dust. The screen door nearly blew off its hinges when she unlatched it, and, by the time she'd got in the house and closed the door behind her, the sky was darkening, full of ugly-looking yellow-dark clouds that hung down like semi-inflated balloons.

I don't ever remember seeing the sky look like this. Like the end of the world. Oh, hurry up, Mom. She went into the living room, sat down and picked up the TV remote control. She flicked down the channels. Talk shows, soaps, game shows. They all seemed completely meaningless in the face of what was waiting for her in the bedroom.

She switched the TV off and reluctantly began to walk upstairs. Climbing the stairs was a challenge, almost like Everest. It was as if, in spite of all the closed windows, the wind had got inside the house and was pushing her back. She got to the top and forced herself to walk along the hall to the familiar door at the end, with the sign on the outside: DISASTER AREA. HARD HATS TO BE WORN. The sign had new meaning today. She pushed the door open.

The dollhouse stood on the desk, just where she had left it two hours ago. Nothing had changed. Well, how could it have? Yet, as she approached the desk, she sensed the energy, coiled like a spring, ready to explode into action. She forced herself to sit down at the desk.

Pray, Granny Pargeter had told her. She tried. But it seemed as impossible to do as that night when she'd been so mad with her cousin.

Please help Peggy, she managed to say.

And: *Let Arthur Blair rest in peace*.

The Celine doll stood where she had left it, by the stairs in front of the main entrance to the Castle Tourmandyne. She picked it up and ran her finger idly around the outline. It really *did* look remarkably like Peggy.

What would happen if there were a *Marg* doll? Would it mean that she'd be part of Peggy's dream world, able to help her? It was worth trying. She couldn't unmake anything, it seemed. But maybe she could introduce a new character.

In the wastebasket by the desk were the cardboard cut-out remains. If she could make a doll to look enough like herself . . .

She used the Celine doll as a model to trace around, and she cut out the figure. White and faceless, it could have been anybody. With her crayons she coloured the dress green and the boots brown. It still looked like any old cut-out doll.

It was no good trying to draw her own likeness. She was hopeless at art. Then she remembered her school photographs. Mom had framed the big one, and sent the two postcard-size ones to both grandmothers. Marg had been given the stamp-size ones for her friends. But there were still a couple left, weren't there? She scrabbled through her desk drawer, gave up in disgust and emptied the drawer onto her bed. There it was. Just one left. Lucky.

Carefully she cut the silhouette of the head away from the blue-grey background and glued it to the doll's head. She turned it over and scribbled wiry brown hair on the back, cut a circle and glued it to the base. Now it really did look almost eerily like her. She stood it upright beside the Celine doll, outside the entrance to the Castle Tourmandyne.

She shivered. Will *I* be in Peggy's dream? Will it be my dream too? Or only hers?

You don't have to do it, a voice warned her. *It's not your problem.*

Yes, it is, she replied sternly. Whatever happens, I'll be in it with Peggy. Without letting herself think too much about what she might be in for, she opened the left side of the house and put both dolls carefully in the nursery. She closed the dollhouse. *There.* It was done.

There was the welcoming sound of the front door opening, and Mom's voice. "Are you there, Marg? We're home!" And she ran thankfully downstairs, telling herself that it was only her imagination, that she hadn't really felt the Marg doll move in her fingers as she put it down.

EIGHT

"You haven't said a word all evening. Aren't you going to tell me what Dr. Cummings said?"

Peggy shrugged. Her face looked pinched, Marg thought, and she had dark circles under her eyes.

"Didn't you like him? He's so nice."

"He was okay. He gave me some pills. But what's the point? He can't stop my dreams, can he?"

"No, maybe not. But *we* can."

"It's not your problem, kid."

"It *is*. I care about what happens to you. Mom and Dad care, honestly. And Uncle Terry and

Aunt Christine . . ." Her words dried up, as she tried to imagine Mom and Dad taking a trip halfway round the world, leaving her behind. Of course they *were* there on business, but still . . . She bit her lip.

"You're a good kid," Peggy told her kindly. "But there's an awful lot about life you don't know yet."

I wonder if that's true, Marg asked herself as they got ready for bed that night. The storm clouds had dissipated and it was cooler, with patches of starry sky showing through the tatters of cloud that remained. But there's a lot I *do* know. Stuff Mom and Dad have told me. And Granny Pargeter.

Thinking of Gran reminded her of her prayers and she said them extra hard, especially the "deliver us from evil" bit. Again she remembered to add the name of Arthur Blair to her list of "specials." Why had he taken his own life? What had driven him to that last desperate choice? Because it was a choice, of course. It had to be.

Perhaps nobody had loved him. Or perhaps, like Peggy, he had turned his back on love. Peggy *was* loved, but she wouldn't believe it; for some reason she didn't *want* to believe it and she tried, by being disagreeable, to make sure she wasn't. Poor Peggy . . . Her eyes closed.

It was dark when she awoke. She turned over, looking for the light from the dormer windows, wondering if another lightning storm had woken her. There was nothing to see, not even a faint grey oblong. How weird. Even on the darkest of summer nights, there was always a little light.

She sat up and swung her feet to the ground, and her bare toes touched cold, slippery floor. Where was the rug? She tiptoed across to the nearest window, the one that looked out on the linden tree, and fell over something hard and angular, which bruised her shins severely. She rubbed her legs and stood still, listening, wondering if she had woken Peggy or her parents. The house was incredibly quiet. She couldn't hear Peggy's breathing, the hum of the refrigerator, anything. Her groping hands could make no sense at all of the shape she'd stumbled over. She skirted it and made for the wall, her hands outstretched in front of her. It *was* incredibly dark, almost as if she'd gone blind.

Her fingers found the wall at last, and the shape of the window. It was closed. Now why would Mom or Peggy have shut the window on a hot July night? She felt for the fastening and her fingers encountered the cross bars of small leaded panes. This wasn't her bedroom window. There were no screens. No window seat. Her fingers found a curved metal handle and she pushed it down. The window wouldn't budge. She pressed her face against the panes, but there wasn't a scrap of light outside. It was almost as if the glass had been covered with black paint.

She moved cautiously back to the centre of the room, encountering a dressing table and a tall piece of furniture, like an upended coffin. Shivering, she found the bed and, beside it, a stool with a candle and matches. With clumsy fingers she scraped a match across the box. It flared into comforting light and she lit the candle, held it up and looked around, her heart beating furiously.

Now the upended coffin shape resolved itself into a tall narrow wardrobe. The shape over which she had fallen was an old-fashioned wooden rocking horse, its saddle torn, its tail in tatters. Besides these there was only the dressing table, a wash stand, and four walls with a door and the window she had already discovered.

She held the candle high and stared, her trembling hand making the flame jump, so that the toy soldiers seemed to move jerkily across the wallpaper. Soldiers in red jackets and blue trousers. With black busbies on their heads and muskets over their shoulders.

Her heart began to pound even louder and her hands trembled so much that the candle flame flickered and threatened to go out. She put the candlestick down carefully on the stool and took a deep, steadying breath. It had worked! She was in the nursery of the Castle Tourmandyne. She shivered and rubbed her arms with her hands. Her fingers encountered fabric instead of bare skin, and she looked down at herself. She was no longer wearing the babydolls she'd gone to bed in, but a long white cotton nightdress that reached to her ankles and had long sleeves finished in a frill at the wrist.

She ran over to the window again and, this time by candlelight, examined the latch. She shook the window, trying to force it open. Nothing budged. What would happen if she took something, say the old rocking horse, and swung it at the window? Would the glass break? And what would she see out there? A country landscape of rolling hills and rows of Lombardy poplars, or a grove of oak trees? Or would it be a fly's eye view of her own bedroom, with *herself* lying asleep in her own bed, and Peggy over there in the other.

Peggy! Where was she? The nursery held but the one small, very lumpy single bed; and when she'd woken she'd been alone. Peggy should be here. That had been the whole idea of making a doll for herself and putting it with the Celine-Peggy doll in the nursery. The magic had worked, but not the whole magic. And now she, Marg Pargeter, was alone, except for the enemies of her own imagination, Lady Tourmandyne and the horrible Quentin Harrowpoint, in Castle Tourmandyne.

Quite suddenly Granny Pargeter's voice came to her, tiny and clear, just as it had over the phone the previous afternoon. "There's nothing evil likes so much as destroying goodness and strength and happiness—so take care."

She stood at the window as the candle flickered, sending her shadow leaping around the walls and ceiling of the little room, and felt goose bumps rise on her arms. She knew exactly what it was that lay outside and around Castle Tourmandyne. She knew the meaning of the blackness outside the window. It was ignorance and fear, loneliness and cruelty, greed and selfishness. And she, Marg Pargeter, aged twelve, going into grade seven in September, had deliberately placed herself in this world of wickedness.

"I didn't know," she whispered. "I didn't mean to."

Like a wind slowly whistling around the house, shrilling through the cracks in doors and windows, growing in intensity until it rocked the house, came the sound of laughter. Humourless, bitter, insane laughter.

Marg screamed. She fell to her knees on the uncarpeted floor. She put her hands over her ears to shut out the terrible laughter. She was no longer afraid of the unknown, but of the known. She knew whose laughter it was—for hadn't she invented him?—it was the laughter of Quentin Harrowpoint.

But putting her hands over her ears didn't help a bit. The sound was there, echoing through her own head. There was no escape. She was helpless and she'd brought it on herself. She had nobody else to blame. And nobody to call on for help.

Or had she? "Mom!" she screamed. "Daddy, help! Gran!"

She remembered what Granny Pargeter had said. "Deliver us from evil." She hung onto those words and to the small sane sound of Gran's voice on the phone. They were like a slender life-line connecting her to the real world—if that other world of school and ice cream and running through the sprinkler *was* the real world. Perhaps Castle Tourmandyne was every bit as real. Perhaps she had made it so. Perhaps she was trapped here for ever and ever in a never-ending dream . . .

The laughter increased in intensity until she thought her head would explode. NO! Gran would not approve of her giving up like this. She would not give up. She would not be afraid.

Even as the thought flashed through her mind the laughter died away. So he—IT—fed on fear. Well, she wouldn't give him the satisfaction, so there! She felt his power strengthening again. So she was not allowed to be angry either. He could feed as easily on anger as fear. So what did she have left to fight Quentin Harrowpoint with?

She thought she heard Gran's voice again. *Love*? That was ridiculous. How could she possibly love such a monster? Then suddenly she found herself thinking of the poor young designer of the dollhouse—what was his name? Arthur Blair. She concentrated on thinking of *him*, sympathizing with *him*, loving *him*. And the laughter died away.

As Marg knelt on the hard nursery floor it seemed to her that the walls were growing thinner and thinner, until they were like mist. And the floor was growing misty too. How could it possibly hold her up? On that thought she found she was falling, falling through soft grey cloud until . . .

She sat up in bed with a jolt. Her face and neck were wet with sweat and she was panting as if she'd been running. Through the open window she could smell the sweet odour of the night-scented stock that Dad had planted against the side of the house. She could see the first glimmer of light in the sky beyond the window frame. Birds sang sleepily down in the ravine. In the next bed Peggy lay, her hair spread on her pillow, her breathing even, her face peaceful.

Marg bunched her pillow up behind her back and sat against it, her arms circling her knees. *I did it*, she thought triumphantly. I broke Quentin Harrowpoint's spell over Peggy. Maybe she'll start to get well now she can sleep properly.

Then she shivered and hugged her knees. For this was just one night. It's almost six weeks till Peggy goes back to Toronto, she remembered. Forty nights. Can I face the Castle Tourmandyne every night for forty nights? Can I hold out against Quentin Harrowpoint's evil for that long? Have I got the courage?

She laid her head on her knees. He was going to get stronger. Something inside her told her that quite certainly. This time she had surprised him. Next time . . . After all, who was she, Marg Pargeter, aged twelve, to think that she could take on the forces of evil?

The breeze was cool against her damp body and she pulled the sheet up over her shoulders, staring at the oblong of window, willing morning to come quickly. Her eyes slowly shut and her head nodded against her knees. She mustn't go to sleep again. If she slept, the dream would be back, and she was too tired, too scared. Quentin Harrowpoint would be able to feed on her fear. And this time he would win.

She found herself remembering a detail in the historical stories she loved to read. On the evening before a young man was knighted he would keep vigil. All alone, his armour and sword laid out beside him, he would wait and pray till dawn. Maybe I'm like one of those knights, she thought. And the idea cheered her up.

But I don't have any armour, she thought.
Deliver us from evil.

"Goodness, chick, you look like something the cat dragged in! Did the thunder wake you up?"

"Maybe that was it," Marg said cautiously. Her head throbbed and she felt kind of crummy. "Just the weather."

"I don't ever remember a summer quite like this. Hailstones the size of golf balls out at New Sarepta. And funnel clouds reported at Rimbey . . . well, Peggy, good morning. And how are you today?"

"Fine, thank you, Aunt Jess."

"Sleep okay?" Marg asked lightly.

Peggy looked at her, and an expression of amazement flashed across her face. "Yes, I slept very well, thanks."

"I expect the pills Dr. Cummings gave you are working. I'm so glad I took you to see him."

"Yes, Aunt Jess," said Peggy meekly, but as soon as the girls were upstairs again, making their beds, she tackled Marg. "What did you do?"

"Don't know what you mean."

"Oh yes, you do." Peggy threw down her pillow and marched across the room to the dollhouse. She peered through the windows and then unhooked the left wall. "So, what's this? Why, you've made another doll. It's *you*. You deliberately put yourself in there, didn't you? Oh, you idiot, you complete *idiot*! Why?"

"Because I wanted to help you."

"*Me?*"

"Well, it was partly my fault, wasn't it? And anyway . . ."

"Go on."

"I love you, Peggy. I care about what happens to you."

Peggy turned away and Marg could see her shoulders were shaking.

"Well, you don't have to *laugh*."

"Oh, Marg, you nut!" Peggy turned round and she could see the tears running down her cheeks. Then their arms were round each other and they were hugging.

"I've been so afraid," Peggy said.

"It's all right. We're together now. We're a team."

"No!" Peggy pulled away from Marg and then put her hands on Marg's shoulders. "You're *not* to try it again. I won't let you. It's too dangerous."

"You can't stop me, Peggy. Castle Tourmandyne is my invention. I can go there whenever I want to."

"I'll tell Aunt Jess."

"Go ahead." Marg couldn't help laughing at the thought. "I just can't wait to see her face when you do."

"You beast! Honestly, you can't do it. You mustn't."

"What's it to you, Peggy?"

"Isn't it obvious? I just won't let you run into danger, getting trapped in those awful dreams. I care about you too, darn it, if you must know."

"Thanks." Marg grinned. "That's what I wanted to hear you say. It wasn't so tough, was it?"

Peggy smiled reluctantly back. "All right. You win. So *now* will you stop this crazy experiment?"

She shook her head emphatically.

"I'll tear up the doll."

"I'll make another."

"You mustn't. He's too dangerous."

"I know."

They stared at each other. Then Peggy nodded her head reluctantly. "Okay. We'll tackle him together. Tonight, okay? See if we can get rid of him once and for all."

"Right! The two of us. If only there was a way of making sure that we'd wake up together in the same part of Castle Tourmandyne. I put the two dolls in the nursery together yesterday, but in the dream I was alone. And you didn't dream at all. We must be together, don't you agree? Together we may be strong enough to overcome him. Separately, I'm not so sure."

"We probably have to will ourselves to be there. I didn't know what you'd planned, and I just prayed that *I* wouldn't wake up there last night."

"Can you bear to go back, d'you think?"

"I think so, if you're there too. Knowing I was alone was the worst part. And wondering if I was going crazy. Anyway, if you're prepared to go back . . ."

"It wasn't so bad," Marg lied. "Nothing to it, really."

It was an untruth only said to bolster Peggy's courage, but as the words died away it seemed to Marg that they were sucked into the walls of Castle Tourmandyne. Something within the dollhouse moved and settled, absorbing the lie. Relishing in it.

"What are you girls going to do this afternoon?" Mom asked as they tidied up the lunch dishes. "I can't offer you anything exciting, I'm afraid. I have a committee meeting that won't be over till five o'clock. But I can drop you off at the Mall, if you like. At least it's air-conditioned."

"I don't think so." Peggy looked at Marg. "What do you think?"

"I'm so tired I can't keep my eyes open. I'm just going to be lazy. Maybe grab a couple of winks."

"I go along with that, Aunt Jess."

"It's even more oppressive today, isn't it? That sky looks quite menacing. I think I'll get going before there's a downpour. Anything I can pick up at the store on the way home?"

"A gallon of ice cream would be nice, Mom."

"If I can get home before it melts." She grabbed her purse and made for the door. "Have a nice afternoon, girls."

As the sound of the tires crunching on the driveway faded away, Peggy looked meaningfully at Marg. "Are you really sleepy, or was that just an excuse?"

"I'm beat. I didn't sleep too well last night. I really need to take a nap."

"Suppose the dream comes back?"

"In broad daylight?"

"It isn't broad daylight *there*." Peggy looked up at the ceiling, to where, in their bedroom, the dollhouse stood.

Marg shivered. "My eyes just won't stay open."

"You shouldn't have got involved. It wasn't your problem."

"We've been through this before. We're in it together, okay?"

"Okay. We'll both nap. If we go, we'll go together. If not, no harm done, right?"

"All right." Marg looked seriously at her cousin. "There's things you have to know about *him*. It's important not to be afraid of him. And not to be angry either. He—IT—feeds on negative feelings."

"You can't expect me to love him!"

"Well, yes, actually, I do. Or at least forgive him."

"For what? Marg, that doesn't make a lot of sense."

"I know. I'm not sure myself. I just have this feeling that it's important to forgive him for . . . for being what he is, I guess. For what he stands for. Like . . ." She hesitated and felt her cheeks grow hot. She blundered on. "Like you should forgive your parents for being the kind of people they are, for not being with you when you need them."

In the silence that followed, Marg thought miserably: I've gone too far. I've blown it. I'm so stupid. Now she probably won't talk to me again. And Quentin Harrowpoint will have won.

She looked up, seeing Peggy's face through a pink haze of embarrassment. To her amazement Peggy was smiling. Not a great big happy smile. Rather a sad smile, in fact, but it *was* there.

"You know, Marg Pargeter, for a twelve-year-old brat, you're pretty smart." Peggy hugged her.

They went upstairs, their arms over each other's shoulders, and into the shaded bed-room. It was like a pinky-gold cave, quiet, just a bit stuffy with both windows closed against the afternoon heat. Marg kicked off her sandals and sat on the edge of her bed.

"D'you suppose it would work better if we went to sleep on the same bed? Mine's fairly wide. Unless you think it's too hot to bear," Marg added shyly. After all, Peggy had a whole suite to herself at her home in Rosedale, and had never even shared a bedroom before, much less a bed.

"I think that's a great idea. If we do go through to *there*, we're bound to stay together, aren't we?"

Peggy brought her pillow over, and they lay side by side on top of Marg's bed, their fingers intertwined. The house was very quiet. The refrigerator hummed on and off. Outside in the shade of the garage Hairy Harry snoozed. South of the city the clouds thickened and mounted.

Their eyes closed and their breathing came evenly, slowly. In the whole house the only movement was that of the kitchen clock frantically jerking around the white face, measuring the seconds. 2:01 . . . 2:02 . . .

NINE

Peggy felt Marg's fingers intertwined in hers. They were plump, warm, a little sticky. Then came the familiar fall and drift into sleep. A numbness in which she could no longer feel Marg's presence next to her. Her hand twitched and she almost woke. She sighed and sank deeper. . . .

Into white mist. It surrounded her, close, impenetrable, shapeless white mist. The only solid thing in the world seemed to be the small space on which she was standing. She looked down and saw her feet, in the hatefully familiar black-laced boots, standing on a slab of stone.

A step. Below was another step and, below that, the ocean of white.

She knew, without having been told, that to step off the stone stair would be to lose herself forever in unending nothingness, a no-place without warmth or love or any human contact. As she looked down at her feet the mist, like an incoming tide, crept a little higher until it lapped over the step below her.

She shuffled involuntarily backwards and felt, at her back, the comforting solidity of a wooden door. With her hands fumbling behind her back she felt the shape of carved panels, and her fingers closed over a large metal ring. Slowly she tried to turn it, and her heart leapt, for it *did* turn! She pushed further and it gave under her pressure. She was about to turn and escape from the incoming tide of white when someone pushed the door back again.

Panic overwhelmed her, because she remembered that all this had happened to her before. Because she knew that on the other side of the door was Quentin Harrowpoint. There was nothing she could do to help herself, and there was no one in any of the great rooms or galleries of Castle Tourmandyne on whom she could call for help.

The laughter began.

I mustn't be scared. The thought flashed through her mind. But that's crazy! How could I *not* be. She reeled as the laughter battered her head. Marg said . . . Marg had said "not fear but love." It was impossible. She couldn't do it. She didn't know how.

"I won't let you make me angry. I won't let you make me afraid," she yelled through the carved door. Could he hear? She didn't know, and maybe it was coincidence, but the laughter died down and for a blessed moment it was quiet. And, remembering Marg, she cried her name into the silence.

Marg had been asleep, lying on her bed with Peggy beside her, in the hot July afternoon. Now it was chilly and almost dark. She moved her hand, feeling for Peggy's, and her fingers encountered the coarse texture of a knitted cotton bedspread.

She opened her eyes and knew that she must be back in the familiar nursery of Castle Tourmandyne. But she was alone. In spite of all they had tried to do, sleep had separated her from Peggy. Quentin Harrowpoint had won.

She heard laughter and stifled the thought. He hasn't won, she told herself. I'll find her. He may have been able to separate us physically, but now there's a bond of love between us that he can't break. We *will* win, she told herself quietly, without fear, without anger.

The laughter died away and in the silence that followed she heard Peggy's voice. "Marg, help me!"

She was on her feet, at the window, again wrestling with the immovable panes. Anger rose and she took a deep breath and stifled it. There was nothing to see outside. The blackness she had observed before had changed to a uniform grey. The greyness of the denial of colour, of shape. Of hope.

She shivered, heard the laughter rise, and told herself that there was nothing to fear. It's all in our minds. It's not real. Again came Peggy's cry. "Help me, Marg! I can't . . . I don't know how to. . . ."

She stumbled down the twisting staircase of the tower to the door she knew must be at the bottom. Her hands groped in the darkness, felt for and found the handle of the door. She turned it and felt it swing outwards.

What lay on the other side? This was the "no-place" part of the house, the unfinished centre between the two wings whose rooms had wallpaper and furnishings, doors and windows that opened to the outside. This section did not even have a floor to separate the main floor from the second. It was only a shell, and out there, beyond the door, might only be a gaping space.

She looked and that is what she saw. A whiteness without shape or dimension. A misty white cave at the heart of a glacier. She shut the door quickly and cowered behind it in the comforting dark of the tower stair. In that dark she heard again Peggy's scream and the answering mocking laughter of Quentin Harrowpoint.

No, she thought and then repeated it out loud, which made it seem more real. "No. What I saw then was Peggy's Castle Tourmandyne. The one made of cardboard and glue. My Castle Tourmandyne is real. It's made of bricks and stone and mortar. On the other side of that door is a gallery of polished wood with carved banisters. To my right, when I open the door, is a staircase—a *solid* staircase—leading down to the main floor."

She steadied the picture in her head and went on. "There are oil paintings of horses and battles and stuffy ancestors on the walls of the staircase as well as in the big hall below. Directly at the bottom of the stairs is the lobby. I can walk downstairs and cross the floor to the lobby. I *can*."

She took a deep breath, opened the door and stepped out onto a polished wood floor that stretched into the distance. She turned right and beneath her feet she discovered one stair and then another. Her left hand was on the carved banister, which came into being as she ran her hand down it. On her right were paintings in gilded frames. Her back straight, her eyes directed in front of her, Marg walked slowly down the whole flight of stairs, stairs that discovered themselves, step by step, as her feet moved trustfully down to meet them.

Beyond an expanse of floor as shiny as a

skating rink were the double doors that led to the entrance lobby of Castle Tourmandyne. From the other side of those doors she could hear Peggy's voice. It was tired, hoarse. But at least Peggy could still call out to her. She could hear, too, the laughter of Quentin Harrowpoint, though she could not see him. What is he like, she wondered? The real person, not the cardboard figure she had named. She pushed away the frightening image of what he might *really* be like. I won't think about that, she told herself firmly. Only about Peggy needing me.

It took a dreamtime forever to cross the glassy expanse of floor, but at last she did it, and her hand was on the handle of the door, easing it open. Soon she would be with Peggy. If they could only be together, holding hands, their strength might be enough to overcome the evil.

She had furnished the lobby in her imagination, in that faraway place in the bedroom of the house in Edmonton, Alberta, Canada, in the real world. She had supplied it with a coat rack, on which were hung an assortment of old-fashioned cloaks and coats, and with a bentwood hat stand. With a deacon's bench beneath which lay a muddle of muddy boots, and with a pottery umbrella stand in a hideous design of red, green and purple flowers.

She recognized each of these artifacts as her eye flashed around the small, five-sided room. Then they ceased to be of any importance, for there, his back towards her, his hands on the panel of the main door, stood Quentin Harrowpoint.

Of Peggy there was no sign. But she heard, coming from *beyond* the outer door, a pitiful, weary cry. "Help me, Marg! The mist is rising. Help!"

So I have to face him first, she thought. Alone.

She stood like a shadow among the cloaks and umbrellas, and took a deep, calming breath. No fear, she told herself. No anger. And she thought of Granny Pargeter.

"I'm here, Peggy," she called out, and found her voice was loud and firm. "I'm right here. We're together, Peggy. Don't be afraid."

He whirled about at the sound of her voice. When she saw his face, even in the dim light that filtered through the small stained-glass panes, her resolution faltered. His features were those of the cut-out doll. The brown hair turned up at the collar line. The soft brown moustache drooped over the mouth.

But the face of this Quentin Harrowpoint shone bluish-white, luminescent, like the skin of a dead fish. The lips beneath the soft moustache weren't soft and full, but thin and cruel. When he opened his mouth she could smell his breath, as sour as a swamp. His jacket was unfastened and he had loosened the shirt beneath it so that she could see, encircling his neck, a reddish-purple scar.

But the eyes were the worst. The eyes were straight out of nightmare, out of monster movies. They were deep red. Not bloodshot, but shining

with a dusky red light that seemed to come from
within, the kind of light you might glimpse when
the stoker swings open the door of a furnace.
In the redness she could see only the darkest
despair. The eyes pinned her to the far wall like
a butterfly.

She flinched and tried to turn her eyes away,
but she couldn't. She shut them instead and said
to herself: Deliver us from evil. For this was IT.
This was what Granny Pargeter had been afraid
of. Up until this moment it had only been a
word, used meaninglessly by grown-ups talking
about third world poverty or pollution or even
politicians. It hadn't meant anything.

But this—this was worse than anything she
had imagined. She opened her eyes again. The
nails at the ends of his fingers seemed very
long. They beckoned her, inviting her to come
forward, to be caught in their grasp. But he
didn't move. The weight of his back was still
against the outer door, keeping Peggy out.

It was a kind of stand-off, Marg realized. So
long as she stood at the far side of the lobby, he
couldn't reach her without relinquishing his
hold on the outer door. If he wanted to catch
her, then Peggy would be free to come in. Well,
she told herself, I can stand here as long as you
can, Quentin Harrowpoint!

But Peggy's voice came again. "The mist's rising, Marg. It's going to drown me. I'll be nothing.
I'll be gone."

"No, Peggy," she shouted back. "There *is* no mist. There's a gravel driveway right in front of the castle. And beyond it is grass and big trees, in a line. Can you see them, Peggy?"

"Trees? Yes, I can see trees."

"Hold on to them in your mind. Trees and grass, and a gravel driveway. They *are* there."

The redness in Quentin Harrowpoint's eyes deepened. He was staring at her, or rather at her ankles. She felt a dry feathery touch and, in spite of herself, she looked down.

Snakes. Brown and white zigzags. Orange and white bands. Hooded heads raised. Panic rushed through her like an ice-cold jet and faintly, beyond her fear, she could hear Peggy's voice. "The mist is back. It's up to my ankles now."

"No, it isn't!" She stamped her foot. And the snakes were gone. He wasn't invincible then. But her anger fed him and she could sense that he was growing stronger again.

This time he made her see insects. All her particular horrors. Beetles, black-backed and shiny. Cockroaches, quick as a flash, with long, waving antennas. Scorpions arching their pincers.

I won't hate you, she told the hideous crawling mass. You're only part of *him* and I won't hate him either.

"You're not real, Quentin Harrowpoint. I made you up and I can unmake you."

The laughter came again, echoing off the walls of the tiny room. Laughter filled with despair and pain. So much pain. Marg felt suddenly sorry for him.

"No!" he screamed and staggered from the door towards her, his fingers clawed.

Love, she thought, and he screamed again. "Stop it. Stop it." He was almost on top of her now, and the smell of his breath made her dizzy and nauseated.

Over his shoulder she saw the front door open and Peggy slide ghostlike into the room. She tried to concentrate, *not* on Peggy but on *him*.

"Stop feeling sorry for me," he snarled in her face. "I don't want your sorrow. Or your pity. I reject them. I reject it all."

"Then go away, Quentin Harrowpoint." Marg managed to keep her voice steady. "Leave us alone."

"I can't. You called me. You brought me back. But you can't rename me. I am who I am."

"You wanted me to. You forced us to build Castle Tourmandyne. So you could have a place to be alive in."

"Alive again. . . ." The voice wailed. "But it's not the same. It's never the same."

"Who are you? Why don't you leave? Stop doing evil. Go back where you belong." It was Peggy's voice, and now she slipped past the hideous figure of Quentin Harrowpoint to stand by Marg. She whispered in Marg's ear, "Don't you see, Marg, this man isn't Quentin Harrowpoint. You didn't invent *him*. That's why you have no power over him."

"Then who?" Marg looked at the hideous face, trying to avoid the glare that came from the eyes. She saw again the scar that encircled the neck, hardly visible in the shadow cast by the collar of his open shirt. What was the name of the dollhouse designer? The young man who, for some unknown reason, had taken his own life.

"Why, you're Arthur Blair!"

The figure wavered and the terrible light behind the eyes seemed to fade. At the same time the walls of the lobby shifted for an instant, as if they were no longer made of stone and brick.

"You're Arthur Blair," Peggy took up the challenge. "And it's over."

Marg clasped her hand firmly. "Yes, Arthur Blair. You're free. You can go away. You can rest in peace."

The figure in front of them shook and bent as if it were no more than a reflection in a broken piece of glass. It thinned to a bent line, a point. And was gone.

All about them, the castle shook. The walls crumbled around them. The ceiling sagged and the air was filled with dust. A roaring, like the roar of an express train, filled their ears.

"Quick, Marg. We've got to get out of here. Castle Tourmandyne is falling apart!"

"What is it? What's happening?" Marg's hands were over her ears. The noise of the express train seemed to be coming straight for them. The window by the linden tree darkened and the room was full of dirt.

Peggy pushed Marg off the bed with a thud and rolled on top of her, just as an ear-splitting crash almost drowned the roar of the wind. Marg spat dirt and plaster out of her mouth. It was in her eyes, stinging. She was lying, face down, with a weight across her back and something sharp digging into one arm. What had happened?

The fear of Quentin Harrowpoint—or Arthur Blair, as he really was—had vanished and there was a sense of lightness, in spite of a more real fear and a very real pain. She tried to move, to wriggle away from the suffocating weight on top of her.

"Don't!" she heard Peggy gasp. Her voice was faint, though she was lying right on top of her, her face buried in Marg's back.

"Peggy, it hurts."

"There's glass and tree branches everywhere. And bits of the roof, I think. We're almost buried. If you move it might all come down."

"What's happening, Peg? Is it a war? It isn't the bomb, is it?"

"No, I'm sure it's not that. We'd have seen a light and there'd have been a louder bang."

"Peggy, Quentin Harrowpoint's gone, hasn't he?"

"Yes. He's really gone. I can feel it. There's no more evil."

"The castle collapsed when he vanished. You don't suppose . . . could we have made this happen, whatever it is?"

"Of course not, silly. The other was just a dream, after all."

Was it? Marg wondered. Was it really? This, whatever it was that had happened, seemed to be just as unlikely.

"It's all right, Marg. Just lie still," Peggy's voice was very weak. "Someone'll come and find us soon."

It seemed to Marg a very long time before there was the sound of pounding on the downstairs door. Footsteps on the stairs. Voices in the hall. "Over this end, I think . . . Anyone here?"

"Help!" Marg managed to gasp before choking on another drift of ceiling plaster.

"Good lord! That big tree's come right down through the gable. All right, kids, hold on. We'll have you out in a flash."

There were more voices. Footsteps running. The wail of a siren getting closer. Loud. Almost as loud as Quentin Harrowpoint's laughter. It stopped. Then the intolerable weight was lifted off her back and she was put on a stretcher.

"Mom," she managed to say, as they began the dizzy journey down the stairs.

The stretcher-bearers stopped. "Is your mom in the house too?"

"No. Committee meeting. Home at five."

"That's all right then. Off we go. We'll get you

both into emergency and someone'll track down your mom. Okay? Don't worry about it."

"*Was* it a war? Are we all right?"

Someone behind her laughed, a comforting laugh, not like *his*. "It sure looks like it, doesn't it? Just a tornado. Ripped along the ravine and came up right by your house. Nothing to worry about now."

"Peggy?" she managed to ask. "Is she all right?"

"Your sister'll be fine," the voice said.

My sister, thought Marg. I like that.

"You were both incredibly lucky," a nurse told her later, as she picked slivers of glass out of her legs and arms with tweezers. "If you hadn't got down on the floor at the far side of that bed, that falling tree would have done a lot more damage."

"We'll keep you in here overnight," the intern said. "Just to be on the safe side. Though you look pretty good to me."

"It was Peggy. She pushed me off the bed and rolled on top of me. Can I see her? Is she all right?"

"Later. Not yet. She took the brunt of the weight of that tree. She's got a broken leg."

Then Mom arrived in a panic, and Marg didn't have time to worry about the sore places, and about the pounding in her heart whenever she remembered those bewildering seconds of the train noise and the crash, for making sure that Mom knew she really was all right.

"It only touched down for a short time," Mom told her after they had hugged carefully. "It ripped up a lot of trees in the ravine and then cut across our lawn and tore up the old linden tree. It looks as if a giant's child had a tantrum in the yard. But it doesn't matter. Nothing matters. You're both safe, thank God. I've phoned Dad up north, so he knows not to worry."

"There's a hole in the roof, the nurse said."

"The tree broke the gable end, but that's all. It could have been much worse. A roofer's on his way now to put plastic over it, so the house doesn't get ruined by the rain. Your room won't be habitable until we can get it repaired. When you get out tomorrow, would you like to stay with one of your friends? We've had lots of offers to put you up. Everyone's been so kind. And I've got all sorts of messages for you."

"Could I stay at home, please, Mom? I'd rather. I can sleep on the living room sofa." It seemed important to keep an eye on Mom and Dad, on everything. Quentin Harrowpoint, otherwise known as Arthur Blair, had gone. But one never knew. Not yet. Not for sure.

"Of course you may. If you're certain you want to. It'll be a bit uncomfortable."

"I don't care, Mom. I just want to keep an eye on you. Oh, but what about Peggy? Where'll she sleep?"

"She's going to have to stay in hospital for a few days, until they can put her leg in a walking cast. With luck we'll have your room fixed up by then."

It took Mom and Marg two whole days to get rid of just the worst of the dust, which seemed to have been driven into every corner of the house. In fact, months later, Marg was to find, when she picked up a book she hadn't looked at for a while, that a fine line of dust lay in the hinge of every page.

Mom hadn't wanted her to go near the bedroom before the workmen fixed it. "It's not safe."

"I'll be careful. I just have to go. It's like . . . I don't want to have nightmares about imagining things," she tried to explain, without having to tell Mom the whole complicated story of Castle Tourmandyne, which she couldn't possibly believe in anyway. "If I can just *see* it for myself, I think I'll be all right."

So then Mom let her.

The room was spooky. The floor was deep in a mixture of garden dirt and plaster. The pretty yellow wallpaper hung in tattered strips, and the pictures and posters and her row of china ornaments were all gone. Maybe in the rubble they might find something. It wasn't important. Even her precious collection of dolls . . . Her eyes went to where her desk had stood. The tree had come down squarely through the dormer window and smashed the desk to matchsticks. As for Castle Tourmandyne, it had only been made of cardboard, after all. There remained not a shred of it or any of its inhabitants.

Marg backed out of the room and went silently downstairs, where Mom began to talk cheerfully about redecorating, asking her what kind of wallpaper she would like.

"Whatever you want, Mom," she said vaguely.

"But it's all right now," she told Peggy, when she went to see her in the hospital. "The dollhouse is completely gone. Arthur Blair can't do any more damage to himself or anyone else, poor man."

"I wonder what it was that happened to him—to make him so . . ."

Peggy's voice faded as she remembered. Marg put a comforting hand over hers.

"Don't think about him any more, Peg. He *is* gone," she said again. "And as for what happened to him, I called Gran to say I was all right, and she said she hadn't found out much from the dealer who sold her the dollhouse. It was in a trunk with a lot of old books, he said. Been in the attic of some house for years. He bought it, sight unseen, because there wasn't a key to open the lock. He told Gran it was a bad buy, because he couldn't sell the books. Downright evil, he told her. He'd burned the lot. But he kept the dollhouse. He couldn't see any harm in *it*. There were some old-fashioned clothes in the trunk too, and the initials on them matched the initials painted on the outside. A.B."

Peggy was silent when Marg had finished her story. Marg looked at her anxiously. Her leg was in traction and she was scarred with red slashes from broken glass, but she had some colour in her cheeks and she looked amazingly happy.

"So that really is the end of Arthur Blair," she said slowly. "I hope he's at rest at last."

"I'm sure he is, Peg. I think the tornado was the last bit of evil working its way out. In the lobby of the Castle Tourmandyne, he really wanted to kill us. He might have done it too. The tornado might have finished us off. But you saved me. You saved us both, Peg."

"Forget it. It was *you* who rescued me from that terrible mist."

"Then I guess we're even. Hey, you know something, Peg? Everyone thought we were sisters when we came in, even though we don't look a bit alike. I was just wondering . . . well, I've always hated being an 'only'. D'you think we could . . . possibly . . . ?"

"Be honorary sisters? Marg, I'd be proud to have you for my little sister."

Marg grinned and kicked the metal bed frame. "I *have* asked Mom and Dad about this, and they said it couldn't be their decision, but yours and Aunt Christine's and Uncle Terry's. But they said I could talk to you about it."

"What, for pete's sake?"

"Well, I wondered if you'd like to go on living with us? Not just for the rest of this summer, I mean, but all year, going to school with me and everything. I know it'd mean sharing a bedroom and not going to a private school and all that stuff, but . . . hey, Peggy!"

"Sorry. Hand me a tissue, will you?" Peggy blew her nose and mopped her eyes.

"Did I say something wrong?"

"Of course not, silly. It'd be great. I don't really mind lining up for the bathroom—well, one can get used to it. And I like sharing a room with you."

"So you *will* stay? Fabulous!"

Peggy shook her head. "I'd love it more than you can imagine, Marg. But it's not where I'm supposed to be."

"Supposed?"

"It's like a pattern, I guess. It's hard to explain how I feel. You belong to Aunt Jess and Uncle Greg here. And I belong in Rosedale. With Mother and Father."

"But they don't seem to want you that much." The words came out without her meaning to. Marg blushed. "I'm sorry, Peg. Gee, that was so dumb."

"It's all right. I mean, it's a fact, isn't it? I've been mad at them for years about it. I let it ruin my whole life. I don't know why it took me so long to work out, but I think I've got it straight now. It's not their fault. It's the way they are. And maybe, even if they don't really want me that much, even if they'd be happier on their own, maybe they *need* me. Maybe I'm part of some pattern in their lives that none of us know about yet. Does that make sense?"

Marg shook her head.

"It's like . . . if I'm not there, maybe *they* won't grow like they should."

"But they're grown-ups already."

"That's something I think I learned from *him*—from poor Arthur Blair. Being an adult doesn't mean one's finished with growing. I've got a sneaking feeling that it's supposed to go on happening your whole life. And if it doesn't —if it's stunted or stopped—like Arthur Blair despairing and angry and turning to evil, then the pattern's spoiled. And the spoiling will spread, like a bit of mildew in a basket of berries, spoiling them all. Like the way Castle Tourmandyne took hold of us."

Marg thought about it. "I think I get it. You're pretty smart, Peg."

"*Me*? I nearly blew my whole life. It's just that I was so stupid before that now you can tell the difference." She laughed. "It's been a weird summer, hasn't it? But you—risking yourself to rescue me from the Castle Tourmandyne—really turned me around."

"Hey, Peg, it was the least I could do for a sister. Listen, Mom says the people are coming to fix the roof and our room tomorrow. In a few days the paint'll be dry. So hurry up and get out of here. We've still got a whole month's holiday together and I don't want to waste a moment of it. Okay?"

ABOUT THE AUTHOR

Monica Hughes was born in England and emigrated to Edmonton, Alberta. She is one of the most popular writers for young people on both sides of the Atlantic, and has won more than a dozen literary awards, including the 1981 and 1982 Canada Council Prize for Children's Literature and the Vicky Metcalf Award.

Where Have You Been, Billy Boy?

It's 1908 when Billy, an orphan, is taken in by Johannes, an old man who operates a carousel at the local carnival. Billy can scarcely believe his luck — food, clothing, a warm place to stay and a marvelous collection of wooden animals.

Johannes' mysterious nightly disappearances and his fierce protectiveness of the carousel lead Billy to suspect that there is more to the machine than meets the eye. When Johannes becomes ill, Billy disobeys his instructions and discovers the carousel's secret: it is a time machine that catapults Billy into the future.

In 1993, Billy is befriended by Susan Patterson, who vows to help him return home. But the carousel is in terrible disrepair, and it is locked away in a barn on the neighbouring Welty property — where the Pattersons are strictly forbidden to go! To make matters worse, Susan's parents are beginning to suspect that Billy isn't really the long-lost cousin Susan claims he is, and time is running out...

ISBN 0-00-224389-X
$16.95
a HarperCollins hardcover

■ HarperCollins*PublishersLtd*

INVITATION TO THE GAME

You are invited to The Game...

Whatever The Game was, it had sucked us in. We were totally committed to it. We breathed it; we talked The Game. And, of course, we exercised. Now we could jog twelve miles and climb the brick wall at the end of the warehouse. Our appetites were enormous....

We had left school plump, pale, and more or less unmotivated. Now we were lean and keen. The Game had become our life. Everything we did sprang from some need of The Game. Sometimes I wondered what would happen to us if we never got another invitation. If, somehow, without knowing it, we had failed a test. A week went by. And another...

Selected as a "Notable Book"
by the Canadian Library Association

A *Canadian Bookseller* selection

Selected by *Parents* magazine for their
"Best Kids' Books of 1991"

ISBN 0-00-647414-4
$4.95
a mass market paperback

🕮 HarperCollins*PublishersLtd*

The Crystal Drop

"...a compelling adventure, powerful science
fiction ground in the present..."

— Arlene Perly Rae, *The Toronto Star*

Drought and the hole in the sky have destroyed Megan
and Ian's world. They are alone now except for an
uncle who lives far away. Megan insists that they must
find him.

Together they enter the dangerous world of the
buffalo jump and escape it only to encounter the sur-
vivalists with their dogs and guns. Megan has taken
one souvenir from their home, the crystal drop. This
is the promise of water that drives them on...

ISBN 0-00-647534-5
$4.95
mass market paperback

■ HarperCollins*PublishersLtd*

THE
GOLDEN
AQUARIANS

"A new Monica Hughes is always
a ray of bright light."

— *Quill & Quire*

Walt Elliot used to believe that his father was a hero.
He was the famous Colonel Angus Elliot, in charge of
"terraforming" — the transformation of planets into
needed resources for Earth colonists.

But now, in the year 2092, Walt has joined his father
on the planet Aqua, only to discover that terraforming
amounts to interplanetary exploitation, resulting in the
destruction of the planet's environment and the gentle
amphibian-like creatures who inhabit it.

In a story that pits sensitive, creative Walt against his
technology-obsessed father, Monica Hughes has once
again written a book that gives young adults the power
to believe in themselves and their ideals.

ISBN 0-00-647963-4
$5.99
mass market paperback

HarperCollins*PublishersLtd*